Bird Dog

(Book Four of the Confessions of a Chick Magnet series)

by Jenny Gardiner

Sleeping with Ward Cleaver

"A fun, sassy read! A cross between Erma Bombeck and Candace Bushnell, reading Jenny Gardiner is like sinking your teeth into a chocolate cupcake...you just want more."

--Meg Cabot, NY Times bestselling author of Princess Diaries, Queen of Babble and more

Slim to None

"Jenny Gardiner has done it again--this fun, fast-paced book is a great summer read."

--Sarah Pekkanen, NY Times bestselling author of *The Opposite of Me*

Dear Reader,

Renowned Renaissance sculptor Michelangelo left behind a series of fascinating sculptures known as the Prisoners, *housed alongside his masterwork,* David, *at the Accademia in Florence. These unfinished statues reveal how painstakingly Michelangelo took a block of marble, and through his brilliance and skill, fully formed bodies emerged. There's a sense that these figures are trying to break free from the bonds of the block of marble in which they are permanently suspended.*

Not to compare myself to one of the most masterful artists in the history of the world, but finishing this book felt a little bit like trying to find some sort of workable form in a block of marble. Only this elusive shape was remarkably good at hiding from me. So much so that I finally postponed the original publication date for the book because there was just nothing I could grasp hold of and work with.

I'd finished my last book in this series on my birthday, December 20 and sent it off to my editor. I was thrilled to have a break from writing; my kids would be coming in for Christmas in a matter of days, and it felt like there was a nice stretch of downtime looming ahead, with nothing to worry about and time to relax and enjoy being with family.

That lasted for all of about twenty minutes when I got a message from one of my brothers asking if any of us had heard recently from our father. Alas, several text messages and phone calls later, we found out that he had passed away in his beloved winter condominium in Hawaii—a sad day for us all, but we were certainly grateful that he died where he was happiest and that he didn't suffer.

His passing then launched all sorts of unexpected to-dos that weren't on any previous lists. We needed to close up my dad's affairs, tie up his loose ends, conduct massive purges of his house and condo (he was a hoarder, so this was no small feat), and organize two memorial services, one in each location where he resided. Not to mention the inevitable emotional fallout of losing one's last parent.

Fast forward to late January when my book was due to my editor, and I couldn't wrap my head around it. She generously extended my deadline first by one week, then two weeks, then three, then four. In late February, exhausted on my flight back from helping to close up my dad's affairs in Hawaii, I finally recognized that I simply could not write this book at that time. Not only was I not there creatively, but my middle daughter was going to be married in late March, and lots of wedding-related things were on the horizon that needed my full attention.

Hence, I took the unusual step of postponing this book, which is not an easy thing to do because Amazon doesn't appreciate you changing your mind about such things and tends to punish writers who do. And of course, it meant disappointing readers who had been awaiting the release of the fourth book in the Confessions of a Chick Magnet *series. To be honest, finally accepting that this book was officially stuck was the smartest decision I've made. In hindsight, I should have postponed it back in January, but I'm super grateful to my editor, assistants, and family who were kind, supportive, and patient and gave me the space I needed to get back to a place where I could create again. And I'm grateful to you, my readers, for your understanding and patience.*

As it happens, this new deadline somehow showed up much faster than I'd planned! Isn't that always the case? But finally—finally!—I wrote this book. I hope you'll enjoy it, and I appreciate your understanding that I had to tuck it away for a short while as life got a little bit in the way.

Happy Reading!

Jenny

Chapter One

ELISE Jackson groaned as she stood smack-dab in the middle of Main Street and reluctantly let Candy Kettering tie a blindfold around her eyes.

"Seriously?" she muttered as her thick blond hair became tangled in the knot after a tight tug. "Blindfolded?" She let out a growl. "This bridal party forced-frivolity thing is starting to pluck my last nerve." They were back in her hometown of Bristol, Montana for the upcoming nuptials of a mutual friend.

Candy patted her on the back, which wasn't the least bit reassuring.

"Now, now. Trust me, it'll be fine. All we need to do is follow these directions and all will be right with the world." She held up the sheet of paper and squinted against the bright sunlight to read it. "It says, *Do something intimate with a strange man, then have your picture taken with him and post it on Instagram.* We'll do this, knock out the final thing on the list, and get busy drinking martinis."

At the rate things were going, Elise was gonna need to be two-fisted with those cocktails.

"Can you define 'intimate'? Am I supposed to get down on my knees and give some dude a blow job for the cause?"

Candy laughed. "Have faith, Elise. How long have we known each other? Do you honestly think I'd make you do something like that?" She pulled the blindfold over her friend's eyes, centering it to secure it snugly.

Elise tried to give her a deadpan look even though it was mostly obscured since she was blindfolded. "Let's just say 'no comment.'"

Candy burst out laughing. "Thanks for that ringing vote of confidence." She placed her hands on the shoulders of her former college roommate and steered her over to the street corner, where a group of people had gathered for some reason. "Hugs for Henry," she said aloud as she read a sign tacked onto the lamppost.

"What's that?" Elise said.

"I dunno. There's this sign hanging up with a picture of some cute kid who must be Henry, and people have lined up I'm assuming to hug a couple of handsome men standing at a table. Not sure why. But that seems kinda intimate, no?"

"And doesn't even involve a strange guy's dick in my mouth. It's a win-win if you ask me. Quick—get me in line to hug one of these idiots and let's get outa here. I'm starting to feel claustrophobic with this thing pressing against my eyeballs. And it's so far over my nose I can't comfortably breathe."

They were performing the final leg of a bachelorette party scavenger hunt. They had found themselves blowing up condom balloons with a couple of guys coming out of Nick's Delicatessen, persuading a dad of two small children to sing "Like a Virgin" along with them as they pretended to be backup singers, and asking a sixty-something woman to write sex advice on a cocktail napkin for Jennifer Lipton, the bride-to-be, whom Elise was thinking of disavowing at this point.

These supposedly wacky adventures were part of Jennifer's bachelorette party fun and games extravaganza, all of which only served to reinforce in Elise's mind that she was 100 percent down with a quickie elopement sans all those nuptial-related frills that she had grown completely sick to death of after having attended or partaken in at least ten weddings in the past year alone. That is, if she ever got married, which was about as high up on her priority list as having emergency dental surgery, so a bit of a moot point.

Candy kept ushering Elise forward in line until finally, they got up to what must've been the front of it because now some guy was speaking to them.

"Aha, we've got a little Fifty Shades action here?" the guy said.

Ugh, the last thing Elise wanted was for someone to think she was some sort of S&M fangirl.

"Yeah, I'm so desperate for a bit of bondage I even walk down the street blindfolded," she said, snarling her lip. "I was just bummed my friend here left my ball gag back in the hotel room."

"Huh… Looks like you've got yourself a sassy one," the guy said. "You might need to take a crop to her backside and put her in her place."

If Elise could see where he was, she'd whack him on the damn backside with that theoretical crop. What did he think she was—a horse?

"Yeah, sorry. She's a little cranky right now," Candy said, elbowing Elise to play along. "See, we're on a bachelorette party scavenger hunt. My friend here has to do something intimate with a strange man and then Instagram the picture. Because I'm a trusty friend, I'm going to keep it PG-rated and not do anything that would humiliate the poor thing. Besides, she's got a bit of anxiety about this mask obscuring her vision, so please, be gentle."

Elise could hear the guy rubbing his hands together. She felt like a stallion with blinders on about to be auctioned to the highest bidder. And not in a good way.

"Cool, cool," he said. "Just so you know, I don't normally hang out on street corners hugging people, but my friend's kid Henry needs some surgery and they just lost their insurance and can't afford it. So a bunch of us decided we'd do a fundraiser hugging people to raise money to help Henry out."

"Oh my God, that is so sweet," Candy said. "Isn't it sweet, Elise?"

Elise had kind of lost her warm fuzzies over this project. "It is sweet, and I hope Henry gets his day in the OR. Now can we get on with this so I can remove this blindfold before a full-blown panic attack sets in?"

"Your friend's a little testy, eh?"

"In all seriousness, she's not often like this. I think she's officially wedding'd out, and the blindfold was the proverbial straw that broke the camel's back. After this, we can go drink, so we're totally incentivized to get it over with and move on to the real fun."

"In that case, let's do it."

"Oh, but Elise, you should see this cute dog that waddled over to us."

"That's my buddy's dog. His name is Sherlock," the guy said. "That's a good boy." His voice raised in that talk-to-your-dog coo.

She wondered if he'd just leaned over to pet the thing since his voice sounded farther away.

"What kind of dog is he?" her friend said.

"He's a basset hound."

"I could eat him up with a spoon, with those hangdog droopy eyes and the ears—Elise, they go all the way to the ground!"

"Awww, man! You know I have to pet the dog now.

But now I can't even find where he is." She pursed her lips, trying to figure out the logistics. "Here—help me so I don't fall flat on my face." She reached out her hand to steady herself on her friend as she bent down. Candy guided her hand to the dog's head. "That's a good puppy." She puckered up her lips and let the dog lick her face as she made kissy noises to him while he slurped his tongue along her cheeks. At last, she stood up, dusting her hands off on her jeans. "Okay, now let's get this over and done with so I can actually see the dog and give him the proper attention he deserves." She paused, her hands on her hips. "How exactly does this work?"

"Well normally when two people hug, one reaches out opened arms and wraps them around the other person, whose arms are also extended. They clasp, hold tight, then release."

"Oh, we've got ourselves a real rocket scientist here today," she said with a smirk. "All righty, then. Arms open wide." She spread her arms out. "Let's hurry up and insert Tab A into Slot B already and get outa here."

A warm body pressed up against hers in a manner she hadn't felt in far too long. Strong arms snaked around her torso, pulling her in tightly. Against her better judgment, she sank into his hard chest—how could she not? He felt so very yin to her yang. But yikes—was that... his Tab A suddenly nudging its way in the general vicinity of her Slot B? Because whoa, that was so not okay. Even though it felt kind of like Old Home Day for some bizarre reason. But no, she could not be pressed up against a stranger who was rapidly growing a hard-on. In broad daylight. Without her even seeing the guy. Ewww. Even if he did have a supposedly cute dog.

Elise stiffened at the, well, stiffness, diplomatically pulling back from the man before he embarrassed himself

5

on her, or worse, she embarrassed herself right back by being more receptive than the occasion dictated.

"Okay, then," she said, shoving her hands in her pockets, making it clear the touching thing was over. "Am I all good to take this blindfold off, Candy? Let's get that picture and vamoose."

Candy worked to loosen the tight knot behind her friend until Elise was able to draw it over her head. She squinted and rubbed her eyes as they were accosted by brightness, then opened them to see standing before her the man who owned the most primo, A-number-one piece of real estate on her permanent shitlist ever: Wilson T. Montgomery. The high school boyfriend who took her virginity then dumped her in the douchiest of ways, leaving her reeling and weeping and cursing the very soil he walked on for years afterward.

"You!" she said, her eyes widening as she pointed at him as if fingering a criminal. "How dare you touch me with your grubby little paws?" She grimaced for emphasis and pointed southward toward his crotch. "Not to mention that *thing*!"

"Elise?" he said, his brows furrowed as he stared at her. "That was *you* beneath the blindfold the whole time?"

"Oh my God, I can't believe you touched me with your, your, your *cooties*!" Not above making a scene, Elise shrieked.

He lifted a brow. "Cooties? What the hell are you talking about?"

"You know damn well what I'm talking about." She grabbed for Candy's hand. "Let's get out of here. Now!"

"Wait a second," he said. "You can't leave yet."

"Why not?"

"Because you have to pay up." He pointed to a woman who sat nearby with a cashbox. "That'll be fifty bucks."

"Fifty bucks? To hug the guy who ditched me on prom

night for slutty Shannon Cadbury, who never met a guy she didn't do on the first half of a date before the entrée was even served? For that matter, even if it wasn't her damn date to begin with?"

He shrugged. "First of all, you are talking total nonsense. Second of all, you agreed to the hug, and we hugged. You did the crime, you gotta do the time." He winked at her and gave her a thumbs-up, which made her want to slug him.

She glared at him as she pulled money out of her wallet and slapped it on the little card table where the cashier worked.

"I'm only doing this so that little Henry gets his surgery. I wouldn't want him to suffer because you're such a knuckle-dragging lout." She lifted her lip in a snarl. "By the way—for what it's worth, hugging you was like hugging a cactus: stiff and prickly."

"Oh yeah? You should be glad you've finally got something good and stiff in your life."

"I'll show you stiff," she said, rearing back as her arm seemed to get a mind of its own, powering the open palm of her hand across his face, with a loud smacking sound like the crack of a, well, crop. "Something I should've done years ago, buster."

With that, she stormed across the central plaza, not even bothering to wait to take the requisite photo to post on Instagram.

Chapter Two

WILL was starting to get into the rhythm of this hugging-for-dollars thing. At first, when his friend Ricardo had suggested it, he laughed it off.

"As if people would pay us to hug them." He rolled his eyes at the notion.

"Seriously, we put a poster up with a picture of Henry with those puppy-dog eyes, I'm telling you women will be on us like white on rice."

Will cocked an eyebrow. "So, are you in this for the philanthropy, or to cop a feel or two with rando women?"

His friend grinned. "Can't we do both?"

They high-fived each other as they figured out the simple logistics to get the project underway. They were all together in town for the next few days for their friend Jamie Gusskind's wedding. Will hadn't been back home to Bristol, Montana for years—his family had all moved away, so there wasn't much of a draw to return. Except of course the breathtaking beauty of the craggy mountains and acres of wildflower meadows dotting the valley below. He'd forgotten how much he'd loved this place and was grateful he'd have a few days to soak it all in before he had to head back to the real world. Although now that he'd returned to Bristol, the real world was starting to lose its luster.

What he hadn't expected with this fundraising brainstorm was his old science teacher from middle school throwing down fifty bucks to hug him, or one of his mother's old bridge partners, who gave him a big squeeze while asking about his folks. Once his father had retired from the National Park Service, they'd followed the sun to Arizona. Having a dad who was a ranger had been pretty awesome while growing up, and as children he and his brother and sister got to enjoy the outdoor life in a way most kids didn't, even in a town where pretty much everyone spent the bulk of their free time—and often even work time—outside, reveling in nature. After the fourth woman old enough to be his mother extracted a hug from him, he leaned over to Ricardo.

"Dude," he said. "Here we thought this was gonna be cop-a-feel day on Main Street. Or at least we'd get the chance to quasi-fondle a couple of women who were easy on the eyes." He scraped his fingers through his wavy, black hair, then scrubbed his hand across his goatee beard. "What do we have to do to get women our age to come over here?"

His buddy nodded toward two women crossing the street.

"If you build it, they will come." He winked. "There's the answer to your prayers, my friend."

Will eyed a stunning blonde, who was maybe three inches shorter than his six-foot build. That was where any comparison with him stopped: where he was hard, she was soft. Where he was solid, she was curvy, with long, lithe runner's legs in tight blue jeans, a narrow waist, and a set of perky tits that filled out her red body-hugging shirt to a T. His gaze wandered to her face, but a blindfold basically covered half of it up, so there was no telling what she looked like under that mask. No matter. He wasn't looking for a date to the prom. He merely wanted to while away the next hour or so wrapping his arms around a bunch of hot women, raise some money, and have some fun, then go drink with his buddies. What wasn't to like about the plan?

"I call dibs on the blonde," he said before his friend got a chance to stake his claim.

"Fine, but you're buying the first three rounds tonight."

Which was kind of a rip-off because Ricardo was technically not allowed to want to grope women since he'd been dating his girlfriend Michelle for at least a month now.

By the time the blonde finally made it to the front of the line, Will had also hugged an eight-year-old girl, someone's cat, and a grandpa. Totally not what he'd anticipated when he signed on for this thing. So having some body-to-body contact with a sexy woman in his age range was a welcome change of pace.

He greeted the blindfolded woman and her guide with a broad smile.

Up close the woman was even more smokin' hot. He was going to have to restrain himself or he'd have his palms all over her gorgeous heart-shaped ass before he knew it. Meanwhile, every word she uttered was so snarky, he immediately wanted to angle his mouth over her smart-ass one to quiet the storm that must've been brewing in her head.

Too bad he couldn't get a good look at her face—between the blindfold and the glare from the sun, it was hard to get a bead on what she looked like. But damn, that body was rocking, with those high, pert tits that were impossible not to ogle and the formfitting jeans taunting him with her tight, hot little body.

Will gave a quick whistle and his friend's dog Sherlock loped over to where they were talking, and the brunette started oohing and aahing over him. Chicks loved that dog. Then again, who wouldn't? He was convinced that Sherlock was the most perfect four-legged creature he'd ever encountered.

The women loved on Sherlock for a bit but seemed in a hurry to get on with the hug. The blonde stood up and asked what was next, so he told her the drill. Maybe he was being a bit of a smart-ass himself, but she'd already played that card, so he was following suit.

When she finally piped down and he slid his arms around her waist, the weight of the world slipped away from him. Here he was, embracing a woman he didn't even know, but he had this burning desire to do exactly what she'd snarkily joked about to him not fifteen seconds ago: insert his Tab A into her Slot B. It did not help matters that the closer his body insinuated itself up against hers, the more his, er, moving parts shifted, like a tree bending toward the warm sunlight.

Shit, what a time to get a hard-on. There was no distracting himself with math calculations or mental images of his sister's wedding, not even imagining the gnarled, arthritic hands of his nana could do the trick this time. Because all he could think about were her soft tits pressed so close to his hard chest, with only a millimeter or so of fabric keeping them from being skin to skin. And if things were different—like, say, if he even knew this woman, right about now he'd be groping for the button at the waist of her snug jeans, tugging the zipper down, and before either of them could count to ten, he'd have been pressed so deep inside her, their heads would be spinning. So strange—how could he be overreacting so much to this woman he didn't even know?

He was vaguely aware of the brunette nearby popping off a bunch of pictures of them on her phone, but he didn't give a care about that. As long as she wasn't Instagramming pictures of him naked, it was all good.

Inexplicably, though, the mood shifted, and the blonde peeled back suddenly, retreating from his tight, warm, embrace, instead backing away like she'd touched a hot stove. Shit. Clearly his physiological reaction had spooked her, which was kind of sucky because it's not like he willed himself to grow hard while pressed up against her. *Hard not to.*

Lost in thought and focused on minimizing his liabilities, he barely realized what was going on until he saw the blindfold drawn away from her face.

"You!" she shrieked, pointing at him accusatorily. "How dare you touch me with your grubby little paws? Not to mention that *thing!*"

Thing? Hardly the most flattering reference to his favorite body part and lifelong bestie.

"Elise?" he said, his brows furrowed as he stared at her. "That was *you* beneath the blindfold the whole time?"

What the what? Elise Jackson? The woman he lost his virginity to? The one who flipped her shit at him halfway through prom night when she accused him of banging Shannon Cadbury? Even though what he was actually doing was comforting her after something traumatic had happened with her own date? And wait a minute—Elise, a blonde? When did that happen? Shit, she looked damn sexy as a blonde.

Well, it was no fucking wonder he wanted to have this woman. And why his dick responded to her like some Pavlovian dog. All these years had passed and yet still, something about her called to him. Even though they'd parted ways practically as enemies so many years ago—she, unwilling to hear any reason, he, sick and tired of trying to get through her thick skull and finally giving up. And now this.

Before he had a minute to process exactly how best to negotiate some sort of it's-been-seven-years-let's-start-again kind of truce, the woman wound up slapping him across the cheek. Damn. He wasn't sure which was crazier—that he stood there, not responding to what she'd done, his hand pressed to his smarting face, or that all he could think about was if this was the price to get her back, then maybe he was willing to pay it.

Chapter Three

"OH my God. I need a cigarette," Elise said.

Candy did a double take, squinting at her. "Whaaa? You don't even smoke!"

Elise rolled her eyes. "No kidding. I hate cigarettes. But that stupid man makes me want to do something reckless, and it's the first thing I could think of and least immediately dangerous."

"How 'bout we opt for getting stinking drunk instead?"

"Duh. That goes without saying at this point. It can't happen soon enough."

She was so ticked off she was practically seeing spots. Or maybe that was from going from being blindfolded to bright sunlight with the addition of intense rage. Either way, she was livid and there was no calming her down.

"Did you see that little rat fink?" Her voice had elevated to Vienna Boys' Choir soprano level. Her eyes were set in a squinty glare. "That disgusting smirk on his face. How dare he touch me like he did?"

Candy lifted her brow. "Umm... don't shoot the messenger here," she said, raising her hands in surrender. "But I'm pretty sure we willingly volunteered you for the task."

"Wait a minute. Whose side are you on?"

Her friend's eyes opened wide. "Dude! I didn't know there were sides involved here. I mean, if there are sides, of course I'm on yours. But I'm super unclear about what happened there. Just sayin'."

They finally arrived back at the hotel where the bachelorette party festivities were underway.

Festivities my ass.

This day had gone from cheesy bridal frivolity to an unwanted reminder about why she left this town behind and had planned on not looking back as much as possible. The only silver lining to this day was that she hadn't given the guy a blindfolded blow job. Which reminded her… what was up with that yearning sensation she'd experienced when he'd embraced her and pressed himself against her so intimately?

On the one hand, she was pissed about it, but on the other hand, damn, she'd be a lying dog if she didn't admit to being at least a little bit turned on. Of course, at first, she freaked out because it was a strange man horning on her, but then she double freaked out when she realized it was her nemesis who'd made his feelings abundantly clear.

In his defense, getting a hard-on was an autonomic response, so it wasn't as if he up and thought, *Hey, it's Elise. Let me get hard for her.* But come on. Make that *don't* come on. Don't come. Don't come close to coming. And don't come near me.

Gah! She had no idea how to process this unwelcome turn of events.

She heard a cackle of squeals and turned to see Jennifer, as always beautifully gamine-like with her lithe neck and cropped, dark Audrey Hepburn hair. As her former roommate and childhood BFF, Elise knew for a fact that there was never a time when Jennifer looked anything but perfect. Perfectly cute, perfectly pretty, perfectly sexy, perfectly girl-next-door. This would normally bug her, but because it was Jennifer, you just had to embrace her charm

15

and perfection.

"And then she hauled back and slapped him, hard," Candy was saying. Elise turned to see five mouths agape as everyone turned to face her.

"Oh my God, why would she do that?" said a little redhead named Sammi, one of Elise's sorority sisters.

Elise turned to face them. "Okay, so you know I grew up here," she said. "Purely by happenstance we wandered into the town square and I got somewhat involuntarily blindfolded"—she threw the stink eye to Jennifer—"and my 'obligatory bridesmaid intimate act'"—she made air quotes with her fingers—"was to hug this guy who was hugging people for charity. I couldn't see him, so all I knew was this strange man with a cute dog was going to hug me."

"How'd you know he had a cute dog?" Sammi said.

Elise lifted an eyebrow. "Off-topic." She turned back to the group. "So, for starters, he wasn't just hugging me—I could feel this bulge growing in his crotch and oh my God, I'm sorry but that was a little too intimate."

"Are you sure you didn't imagine it?"

Her forehead ski-sloped toward her nose. "There is no mistaking a humongous cock pressing up against your crotch like a missile with a homing device."

"Yeah, but let's be real. It's been so long, maybe it was a mirage, like an oasis in the desert for a drowning man." A grin spread across Jennifer's face and she licked her fingertip and made a tally mark in the air, then elbowed her friend. "Sorry, I couldn't resist."

"First off, it hasn't been that long. And second, even if it has been a little longer than might be normal, it's like riding a bike. You don't forget."

Candy held up her finger. "Hold on, girls. I think we can lay to rest any dispute about this. There's photographic proof." She held up her phone. "I popped off a bunch of pictures so that we could post on Instagram like the directions said."

She navigated to her pictures and scanned the succession of images taken from differing angles until she found the damning evidence. Using her fingers, she expanded the photo till the bulge filled the screen.

"Ay, caramba," she said. "Either that man had a foot-long hoagie in his pocket, or he was super happy to see you." The women all laughed. "I don't know that I'd have slapped him so much as hopped on board for the experience."

Elise growled. "Stop it. This is no laughing matter."

"Awww, come on, Elise," Jennifer said. "Since when did you get so hypersensitive about something that you've gotta admit is awfully funny."

"Since my blindfold was removed and there standing before me with a still-looming lump in his pants was Wilson Montgomery. God knows what he's doing in town, but I'm hoping he rides off into the sunset pronto and I never have to see his face again." She failed to mention that she noticed the beard and found it unsettlingly sexy. Not like she was a facial hair kinda gal, but he had a Lin Manuel Miranda thing going that stirred things up in the pit of her belly, despite herself.

"Or feel his crotch again." Sammi winked at her. Sammi never was her favorite sorority sister. Maybe it was thanks to her complete lack of empathy?

"Why would he be back here after all these years?" Elise said. "I thought his parents moved away long ago."

Jennifer bit her lip, then scrunched her face. "Ummm… There's something I might have forgotten to mention to you."

Elise squinted at her. "No—"

Jennifer nodded, a pleading look in her eyes. "I'm sorry, hon. Jamie thought it best not to say anything. He didn't want to get you all upset and agitated, and he knew you would and, well, I figured you'd be okay with it because it's your best friend's wedding and a lot of time has passed and we've all grown up. Besides, for the sake of our happiness on our wedding day, you'll of course let bygones be bygones, right?"

Elise began to pace, running her fingers through her hair. "You mean he's in town this weekend because he's in the wedding?"

Her friend nodded like a dog being scolded for peeing on the floor. "Ummm... yeah." Elise couldn't help but think if she'd had a tail, it would be tucked neatly between her legs right about now.

"Your acts of omission are killing me here." Elise thrust out her lower lip. "Because all of a sudden I know what you're not telling me is that not only is he in the wedding, but he's also the best man. Which means that he and I—the maid of honor—will be paired up together, which means I am so going to kill you. But I'm going to do it real slow. With a butter knife. Carve you up into teeny, tiny pieces and feed you to the coyotes."

Jennifer had flagged down a waitress who reappeared with a tray of margaritas. Jen grabbed one and thrust it into her best friend's hands. "Nothing a little liquor won't make all better, right?"

Elise put the salted rim to her lips and tipped the drink back quickly, guzzling the thing in about three gulps. She immediately reached for another drink on the tray. "Just so you know, no amount of liquor will make this better. I've been officially relegated to the seventh circle of hell for the next several days, and you are going to owe me for the rest of your life."

Jennifer smiled. "On the other hand," she said, "maybe time has healed old wounds. You and Will might hit it off again. After all, you two did have great chemistry."

She shook her head. "We didn't have great chemistry. We were in chemistry class together."

Jen waved her hand. "Oh please, the smoldering looks you two exchanged. The heated make-out sessions at barn parties. I seem to recall you two disappearing up in the haylofts plenty of times."

"Who didn't? That doesn't mean anything and it doesn't fix what he did."

"If you ask me, that rock-hard hoagie could go far to fixing things," Sammi said.

"Jesus, Sammi. Do you have dick-on-the-brain disease or something?"

"I'm just saying, wowza. If he had that reaction when hugging you for a few seconds, imagine how great it would be if you were a willing participant."

"But I wasn't a willing participant. I was a standing piece of deadwood and that's how I shall remain."

"I don't know, Elise," Jennifer said. "I've heard he's got quite the stable of women who have been more than pleased by his, um, hoagie."

"Oh, well, in that case, that makes him all the more tantalizing. He's a disease factory hooking up with any woman with a pulse. Of course, that sounds exactly like the Wilson Montgomery I ditched years ago, the two-timing son of a bitch."

"Someone call my name?"

Elise turned around to follow the sound, and damned if Will wasn't standing there, looking downright edible—that is, if he was some sort of toxic plant, like, say, those mushrooms you pick in the woods that cause your kidneys to shut down if you ingest them thinking they're good for you.

In reality, she couldn't lie to herself—the truth was he looked amazing. He'd filled out over the years, and he clearly worked out, his cut biceps straining against his T-shirt, his chest looking like it needed to be pressed up against. Yet again, nope. She could not go there. Never again with Will Montgomery. She'd sooner have a combination lobotomy, tooth extraction, and a hundred stitches with no painkillers than go mano a mano with that boy. But man... oh... man... he sure looked darned good.

Man, oh... whatever.

Chapter Four

IT escaped Will why Elise was still clinging so desperately to that bizarre story she'd concocted all those years ago at prom. Why ever would any sane man give up someone like Elise for anyone, let alone that sad, lonely, unkempt Shannon Cadbury, who he liked as a friend and for whom he had a great deal of compassion, but zero interest in romantically, then or now. Hell, he didn't even know what happened to her since everyone graduated and moved on with their lives.

Evidently for Elise, time had not healed old wounds, and she seemed hell-bent to inflict some of those wounds on him just for good measure. Just like old times. The good news was he wasn't going to play those games anymore. Sure, he might have some fun toying with Elise because she was so damn dug in, but he refused to emotionally engage with this stuff ever again. Been there, done that, got sick of pounding his head against the wall. He wasn't, however, sick of banging *her* up against the wall in the hayloft, but he figured that wasn't going to be on the menu over the next several days. Shame, that.

He fondly remembered the two of them experimenting as young lovers learning their way around one another's bodies. Boy, had her figure only improved with age. He tamped down the memory of him plastered up against her only hours earlier and wished that things could be different.

Such a shame she held on to a grudge so damn long. Especially considering it was a wrong grudge to begin with! But he'd tried hard to persuade her of that back in high school and she refused to see the light. Oh well. Her loss. There were plenty of other fish to fry, and he'd spent the past few years gladly cookin' 'em up. Even though he'd dearly love to sauté up something more enticing with her.

He decided to fuck with her some more.

"Will Montgomery, best man for the weekend's festivities," he said, extending his hand to shake hers. "Pleased to make your acquaintance."

Elise grimaced, her eyebrows furrowed so far toward her nose she looked as if she might be in physical pain. Though he knew in her warped mind, he was her pain. At least she was cute when she was angry, resting bitch face and all. Well, not a resting bitch face, more like bitching bitch face. He nodded at her. "Aren't you going to introduce yourself to me?"

She glared at him, still not proffering her hand.

Will glanced at the rest of the bridal party, who seemed to be enjoying their drinks based on how rapidly they were throwing them back. "Ladies." He nodded at them.

"I'm Sammi Ferguson," a little redhead said as she reached out not one but two hands, clasping his with hers and not letting go. It looked like she was staring at his dick. He rolled his eyes at her brazenness. Kids these days. "Hard to meet you."

He cocked his head. "Hard to meet me?"

Her eyes grew wide, then she reached a hand in the air as if to erase something on an imaginary whiteboard. "Oh my God, I'm so sorry. I said that wrong. I meant to say 'glad to meet you.'"

He lifted a brow and decided he didn't want to pursue

that anymore.

"Will! So great to see you!" Jennifer reached over and gave him a hug.

"Glad someone's happy to see me," he said, shaking his head.

"Honey, I'm more than happy to see you," the redhead said, sizing him up from head to toe. Weird—he couldn't help but feel she was mentally undressing him. On the one hand, this could make things super easy for him this weekend. On the other hand, this could make things super complicated for him this weekend. Red seemed ready and willing. But he knew he was being judged—even if it didn't matter to him—by the same tall blonde he couldn't help fantasizing about. One last go-round before the weekend was out would be perfect, but banging her fellow bridesmaid would not contribute toward that elusive goal.

Jennifer stuck a can of Going to the Sun IPA in his hand. "Here. Drink. Now."

"If you weren't getting married in a couple of days, I'd marry you," he said, giving her cheek a gentle squeeze as he opened the can deftly with his other hand.

"Except that I'd have to kill you," a nearby voice said. Will turned to see his best childhood friend Jamie walk up and kiss his bride-to-be.

Will held up his hands in surrender. "Trust me, I'd never step on your turf, dude. What's yours is yours and what's mine is—" He clenched his hand a little too tightly around his beer can as he noticed Elise chatting up some guy he vaguely recalled from high school who looked like he thought could get into her pants with ease. It made him slightly crazy to the point that he suddenly wanted to punch the guy.

"What's yours is what?" Jamie said, scraping his sandy

blond hair back from in front of his green eyes. His gaze fell where his friend was looking. "Aah… You mean what was yours isn't yours?"

Will glared at him. "Not for lack of trying."

Jennifer slung her arm over his shoulder. "The good news is that's all in the past, and this weekend we'll all be in the best of spirits and there will be no drama. Right?"

"Have you ever known drama to follow me anywhere?"

Jennifer pursed her lips and nodded toward her friend. "Only when it came to Elise. Good thing that is from another chapter long, long ago. Nothing to see here now. Move along." She waved her hands as if shooing away a pest.

Will nodded as he took a hard slug of his beer. "Not one damn thing." He cleared his throat. "Now who's ready to party?"

Will couldn't help but notice Elise wasn't without a rapidly depleting drink in her hand over the next few hours. Nothing good was going to come of that. At some point, she was going to go from holding her liquor to spewing it, and that moment was gonna be ugly. All night long, he'd respected Jennifer and Jamie's wishes and kept to himself, deliberately not interjecting himself into her business, or even trying to toy with her like he'd started to earlier in the evening. As much as that would have been his inclination, this was their weekend, and he needed to respect that.

But when he glanced over again, he saw that aggressive douchebag—what was his name? Tad, Tod, something like that? And wasn't his nickname in high school Bird Dog because he was relentless in trying to sleep with as many girls as possible? He had cornered Elise and had started fondling her. That's where Will drew the line. Elise was too drunk to be on the receiving end of the hard press from some asshole, and it was the gentlemanly thing to do to protect her from his unwanted advances. Well, he sure hoped they were unwanted, at any rate.

"I'm giving you a split second to remove your filthy fucking hands from her ass," Will said as he reached for Elise's hand and tugged her toward him.

The guy frowned at him. "Beat it, asshole. She's mine."

Will turned toward his former girlfriend, his brow lifted in question. But the unmistakable haze of alcohol intoxication was clouding her eyes and he knew she wasn't in the right condition to defend herself against this dickhead. "No more chances. Get the fuck away from her, or you'll regret it." He gave his best snarl as he put his arms around Elise. He leaned his head toward her ear. "You okay?"

She nodded, forcing out a slurred sentence. "I can take care of myself, thanks."

He rolled his eyes and pulled her the rest of the way from the Tad or Tod, the Bird Dog, who must've decided the shit-faced bridesmaid wasn't worth the effort.

"C'mon," Will said. "Let's get you to bed."

"With you? Fat chance." Elise stuck out her tongue at him.

"Don't tempt fate by your actions, sweetheart."

"You should be so lucky." Her breath smelled a little like a fraternity house on a Sunday morning.

"You're not telling me anything I don't already know. Now, come on. You'll thank me in the morning."

"No." She folded her arms across her chest and thrust out her lower lip in a masterful toddler-tantrum pout. "I wanted to go home with what's his name." She aimed her thumb over her shoulder toward the bar, where she had been standing with what's his name minutes earlier. "Besides, you don't even know where I'm staying."

"I'm not even going to dignify that foolish wish with a response. You've got two choices." He held up his hands, first extending his pointer finger. "You can tell me where you're staying, so I can take you back there before you get into trouble and live to regret it. Or"—he lifted his middle finger—"you're coming back with me, where at least I know you'll be safe."

"Safe like Shannon Cadbury was with you?" He could barely hear it above the noise of the bar, but yeah, he still heard that snide swipe loud and clear.

He shook his head. "I'm not gonna let you push my buttons, Elise. I'm looking out for your safety because you're in no condition to even recognize when your welfare is in question." With that, he leaned forward and scooped her up into his arms, then slung her over his shoulder like a Costco-sized sack of dog food as he marched out of the bar, into the lobby, and punched the elevator button.

"You stupid ape, let me down!" Elise spluttered her half-hearted protest, but even that seemed slurred and unintelligible, so he chose to tune her out as the elevator door opened and he entered. She pounded her fists into his backside, which he tried to tell himself was just a little bit of kinky foreplay; otherwise, he might get annoyed enough with her to dump her out onto the curb in front of the hotel. But it had started to rain so she'd be especially displeased with that. Instead of letting her protests annoy him, he looked up to the mirrored elevator walls and took in the view of her luscious backside in the short white denim skirt she had on. Her legs were trying hard to kick him with her beat-up cowboy boots, but he had a firm grip on her so he could take in the scenery without skipping a beat.

He let out a loud whistle. She paused in her protestations.

"What was that for?"

"Oh, nothing much," he said.

"If it was nothing, you wouldn't have whistled. What is it?"

He shrugged. "Just taking in the sights is all."

She tried to reach around him to see what he was looking at, but the elevator stopped and the door opened before she managed to twist herself up, which was fine by him. He knew she'd only flip out on him if she saw what he'd seen. He was already gonna catch holy hell from her for what he was about to do.

"Where are you taking me?"

"I told you, I was taking you out of the line of fire for a while."

"I am so not going to your room and letting you take advantage of me."

"Elise Jackson, you may not think much of me anymore, not that I have any control over your thoughts, but one thing I know you know is that I am not a man who would take advantage of a vulnerable woman."

She muttered, "You sure did with Shannon Cadbury."

Will took a deep breath and muttered a mantra under his breath. "I am not going to react. I am not going to react. I am not going to react." He pulled out his room key and pressed it to the keypad, turned the handle, and kicked open the door.

"Quite frankly, now that I've gotten you away from that asshole Tad, or Tod, or whatever—and did you know he gave a couple of girls chlamydia our senior year?—I'm sure you're going to be just fine. But if I were you, I'd take advantage of things and sleep it off right here. I'll have the bottle of Advil at the ready for you come dawn when you're hating yourself for the wicked-bad moral hangover I'm sure you'll experience, not to mention feeling like you got run over in a cattle stampede."

He plopped her down on the bed and helped her out of her boots, then pulled the covers over her, turned out the lights, and went into the bathroom to get ready for bed himself.

By the time he slipped out of his clothes and slid beneath the covers on the other side of the spacious king-size bed, she was snoring away. He turned his back to her, put a pillow over his ears, and inhaled deeply. Damn, there were times in his life when he'd have practically gotten off at the mere thought of spending a night in bed with Elise. Back in high school, their fooling around options were catch-as-catch-can, wherever they could steal a little uninterrupted time and space. After all these years, here she was, and here he was. But she was passed-out drunk and would wake with a bucketful of regret, no doubt ready to blame him.

The only fun thing was that he knew it would make her crazy tomorrow wondering if she actually did anything with him before she blacked out. And maybe, for the fun of it, he could keep her guessing.

Chapter Five

ELISE woke with a start from a dream in which she was straddling her ex-boyfriend Will Montgomery in an elevator, of all places. Wherever that idea came from, her brain was too fogged to decipher. Her mouth was so parched it felt like the dust bowl from the Great Depression. And she had to pee so bad her molars were almost floating. She'd barely spent a minute in her room after check-in that morning, so the landscape of the place was kind of unfamiliar to her. She fumbled her way to the bathroom, filled a glass to the top and guzzled it down, then another, then peed. She spotted a bottle of Advil on the counter—Wow! She had the presence of mind to get that ready!—and knocked back three pills with another swig of water.

She was crazy hot, so she stripped off her shirt and skirt, unhooked her bra, and made her way back to the bed and slid beneath the top sheet. She was probably still drunk after all those shots and cosmos and margaritas she'd consumed.

Note to self: no more liquor for at least the next half a day.

She rolled to her other side, only to find herself making skin-to-skin contact with a man. What? Good Lord. Had she gone back to the room with that big burly cowboy she knew back in high school, the one who'd flirted with her all night? And if so, had she done anything? Impossible—she'd still had her clothes on, right? Unless they'd worked their way around them in the heat of passion or put them back on afterward. Her recollection of what had happened after the sixth cosmo was pretty much zero. But she knew this man felt warm and hard and damn, maybe she ought to make up for lost time in case she hadn't done anything—if, God forbid, she'd come back and passed out when he was expecting her to be randier. Besides, she'd promised herself she was going to let it all go and have fun at this wedding. Work had been stressful, and frankly, coming back to Bristol had been too.

She wrapped her arms around him so that her breasts pressed up against his back, and her hands skimmed along his chest and abs. Hmmm… he had an amazing body. Broad shoulders, smooth chest, solid abs. And, oh, wow, her hands slid lower only to find there was no waistband beneath which she could slide her exploring fingers. Commando? Yowza. Well, if she was guilty of failure to launch last night, maybe it was time for a little middle-of-the-night romp. After all, she'd vowed to let loose this weekend: what better way than to do this?

Her hands moved lower, circling his sleeping cock as her lips pressed along his shoulders. She heard him groan softly in his sleep. He was going to need to do better than that. Slowly, she slid her hand along the rapidly hardening appendage, and like magic, it grew as she played with it. This was kinda fun, a sneak attack in a pitch-dark room—it was sort of mysterious.

She knew someone who'd dated Tad—oh crap, was it Tod?—back in high school, and she remembered hearing he had quite the libido. Perhaps it would be a good change of pace for her to throw a little caution to the wind. After all, she'd be out of here after the weekend. No need to worry about anything after the wedding was over. A little fun in her otherwise boring life, then back to DC to the job she didn't even like anymore, but that was something to worry about for another day. Right here, right now, she was going to seize the moment and not look back with regret.

She inched her way down the bed and shifted herself around, slipping completely beneath the blanket, half-rolling Tad/Ted/Tod toward his back as she planted kisses starting along his quite lovely hard ass, over his hips, half-kissing, half-licking a trail toward where her hands had been busy warming him up. When her mouth finally found his cock, she stroked her flattened tongue from base to tip and licked along the rim before taking the head into her mouth. God, she felt so subversive doing this, practically stranger sex, in the dark. It was so out of character, but it was kind of fun, a little sneaky even.

She leaned forward and situated herself, elbows planted on either side of his hips as her mouth slid down the length of his cock, engulfing it with her lips, her teeth, her tongue.

"Oh, fuck, Elise, don't stop." She heard the moans from above, somewhere beyond the blanket, which gave her a nice privacy barrier to keep on doing what she was doing. She slid one hand from the base upward, meeting her mouth as it slid back down. She could feel his hips start to grind, pumping himself toward her eager mouth.

"Oh, babe, I want you so badly."

And she wanted it just as badly, if for no other reason than that she hadn't had it for so damn long. Yet she kind of wanted to keep playing this anonymous sexy little game, cloaked beneath the cover of darkness.

She scooted over enough to give him room to settle behind her and position himself at her opening, already wet and ready.

"I want you to take me like this."

She could hear the voice, still bleary with sleep but

rapidly waking. "Are you sure about this?"

"Don't give me a reason to reconsider." She pressed herself up against him, and he complied.

He slid his cock along her slick center, circling several passes around her clit with the swollen head before finally pressing it to her opening. They both moaned as he slowly slid into her, and she gasped at the feel of his swollen cock as it filled her. She'd lost track of how long it had been since she'd had sex with a man—it had been at least a year since she'd stopped dating that boring guy Jim from accounting. And sex with him was so tedious that it hardly even counted. But it was like riding a bike, right? Surely she could go from rusty to orgasm in no time flat. He held still, balls deep inside of her and Elise bit her lip at the simmering pleasure, then reached down between her legs to rub herself. That's all it took before the familiar tingling rose through her pelvis, splintering through her body as Tod/Tad/Ted thrust deep inside her and froze right there as he came apart, pulsing into her warm body as he collapsed on top of her.

For a few peaceful moments, only their labored breathing pierced the silence of the dark room. Until he shifted enough to roll off of Elise and turn her toward him, planting his mouth over hers.

"That was amazing, babe," he eventually said. "I'm so glad you finally came to your senses. To think we've missed out on this for all these years."

All these years? Not like she and Tad/Tod/Ted ever had a "thing" they'd have been missing out on. Sure she kind of led him on to piss off Will back in high school. But there was no history between the two of them, so what the hell did that even mean? Oh well. It was late and she was adequately satiated and ready to pass out cold after that lovely little prehangover orgasm. She'd have plenty of time to figure that all out in the morning.

"Shhhh," she said, pressing her finger to his lips. "Sleep."

Remarkably he complied and she curled up in his arms, her back to his chest, and quickly drifted off to sleep.

Blackout shades. That's what this room needed. Something to keep the invasive rays of the morning sun from piercing her eyeballs' meager defenses. What good were eyelids if they didn't block out brilliant daylight? Good God, it made her eyes ache, which made her brain ache, which made her whole being ache. Since when did a little sunlight assault your entire existence like this?

And then it came back to her in tiny vignettes: her drinking enough liquor alone for the entire grouping of bridesmaids. Jesus, Elise's head felt like she had a stone carver trying to work his way out of her cerebellum, hammering away with a rhythmic thumping that Elise swore she could hear. She tried to open her mouth, but it felt glued shut.

Christ, wasn't it the bride, not the maid of honor, who was supposed to be so hungover after the bachelorette party that she needed a team of sled dogs to haul her out of bed? She felt movement behind her and glanced down to see two hands pressed possessively to her breasts, and she arched a brow. Ummm… What the actual fuck? She hadn't brought a date with her to Bristol this weekend. She hadn't even been with a man this way in longer than she could remember— easily a year. *Crap, crap, crap, crap, crap.* Her eyes grew wide when she then felt the unmistakable press of a hard-on

33

against her bare bottom. This was impossible. How could she be naked, very possibly still slightly drunk, with tundra-like levels of dehydration, when all she'd done was attend her best friend's bachelorette party?

In her morning-after fog, she tried to recall the sequence of events from the night before. She remembered drinking a few margaritas. Then maybe a few cosmos. She'd lost count of the tequila shots she'd ingested. Then came a few more cosmos. Maybe a beer or two. And she was talking to that guy—what was his name? Tod? Tad? Ted? He was sorta cute, though he always wore a cowboy hat, which felt to her to be a bit pretentious. Unless you spent your days rustling cattle, it always seemed to Elise like cowboy hats were all about the costume, which usually made her roll her eyes. There's no way she'd have left with him last night. In fact, the only reason she'd have bothered chatting with him much at all was for the same reason she'd done so after she and Will broke up back in high school: to make Will jealous.

Will.

Will?

Will!

Oh, fuck. No way. Not Will.

Shit, shit, shit, shit, shit. Will. Curse Jennifer and Jamie for deliberately omitting the fact that Will was the best man. How had she not known that? How had she not gone over that with Jennifer? Had she just assumed it would've been Jamie's college roommate doing the honors? And last night. That guy Tod/Tad/Ted—he kept squeezing her ass, didn't he? Which annoyed the hell out of her, but she was so drunk she didn't even want to deal with it. Normally she'd have racked a guy in the balls for doing that to her. Wow, she was losing her game. So then what had happened?

She went down her mental checklist: Drinks—lots of

drinks. She remembered at some point her head was spinning—never a good sign. Then that Tod/Tad/Ted dude was groping her. Oh God. Then Will. He came over and got all testosterone-y with the guy, didn't he? And then he insisted that she leave with him. Where did they go? Her pulse started to speed up. He carried her—carried her!—to his room. Had he then stripped her clothes off? How else would she have gotten naked? With Will Montgomery, of all the damn men in the world. How was she going to extricate herself from this prickly dilemma? And what even happened?

Oh God. This was awful. Worse than awful, this was terrible. Make that downright mortifying. Had he taken advantage of her? Impossible—that was so not Will's MO. Had she? Yikes—that wasn't hers either! What had she done? She squinted her eyes shut against the incessant pounding—where the hell was her Advil? Where the hell was she? Was she even in her own hotel room? Without moving a muscle, she scanned what she could see through slit eyes, but it looked like a hotel room—probably quite like the one she'd checked into yesterday, though for the life of her she couldn't recall any details. She saw something on the floor that looked like a black carry-on suitcase, which definitely wasn't hers—she'd opted for the easy-to-find-on-the-luggage carousel polka-dotted one.

So that meant she was in his room. Which made sense since he'd dragged her here. So then what happened? From the bar to the room was basically a blur. She had a vague sensation of being plunked down on the bed like a butcher would drop a big side of beef on the block for carving. There had to have been no seduction, no stripping of clothes, no nothing. She was not in any condition for that—of that she was sure. So, then what? And that's when it started to come to her: at some point in the middle of the night, her bladder was protesting wildly. She got up to pee, staggered to the bathroom. She was so hot—so hot!—so she tugged off her clothes before returning to bed. But what happened then?

She felt like some forensics analyst reconstructing the scene of the crime. The heat of embarrassment overtook her as she added things up: *she'd* been the instigator. *She* was the one who thought it was a good idea to have a drunken one-night stand with some random dude, even though she mistakenly thought it was with an entirely different guy. Someone she'd never have hooked up with sober. *She* was the one who inched down his body and took his cock in her mouth. Oh, sweet mother in heaven. Elise "Will Montgomery is Dead to Me" Jackson had given that very same Will Montgomery a blow job? Not like she'd never done that before—frankly, with him she'd become quite expert at it back in the day since it was easy enough to do in the back of his pickup.

But now with the clarity that came with dawn's light revealing itself to her, she sure as hell couldn't face him. But how could she slip out and pretend nothing had ever happened? She closed her eyes—against the alcohol-induced throbbing in her brain; against the large, warm hands that were covetously blanketing her breasts at this very moment; against the tide of recall that was beginning to slosh ashore in her memories of last night; and against the realization that she probably drunk-fucked the man who broke her heart— the same man she'd promised herself never to have physical contact with again. In her wildest dreams that might have included a handshake, but certainly not penis-to-vagina contact.

Penis-to-vagina contact… Oh dear God. Had she done *that*? With him? *Skin-to-freaking-skin?* Was she mad? In what universe would she have gone without protection? She made a mental note to never ever do a shot of tequila for the rest of her life. And maybe cut back on the cosmos and margaritas by a good 90 percent.

The naked man who was at this moment pressed up to her shifted in his sleep enough to give Elise a chance to slip out of his clutches. Hoping he wouldn't notice, she did a near-dog roll from the bed to the floor, then crawled on all fours around the bed, trying to scrounge up her various articles of clothing so she could dress and run pronto. She was able to put her hands on her white denim skirt, so she lay on the icky hotel carpet flat on her back as she jimmied it up her hips. She stuck her hand in her pocket, relieved to find her phone still in its place. Next came her little satiny black tank top. She silently patted around on the floor for her bra but wasn't finding anything. The sunlight hadn't quite reached this side of the bed yet, so it was too dark to find. She heard him roll over in the bed and panicked. No time for the bra, and she still hadn't found her underwear either. She spread out on the floor on her stomach and did a little starfish crawl, whereupon she found both boots— thank God. She would never give those things up. She slipped her tank on, braless, and decided it was better to leave those wounded soldiers behind than to have to face the music with Sleeping Beauty up there if and when he awoke. She crawled like a commando to the door, not even bothering to don her boots, quietly stood up, undid the latch, and ever so gingerly turned the door lock, then quietly slipped out into the hallway, her dignity and pride having taken a hit, but at least she had enough clothes to do the walk of shame without having to steal anything of his. As far as she was concerned, this event never happened.

Chapter Six

WILL woke to the telltale snick of the door latch, and he immediately knew that meant Elise had pulled a runner. Dammit, he should have insisted on Round Two with her before she'd fallen back to sleep right after that glorious and most unexpected orgasm. Considering this opportunity might never present itself again, at least he could have built up a stockpile for the memory books. It was obvious he'd gotten his hopes up for nothing. It wasn't every day that you awoke to the unexpected sensation of a warm, wet mouth encircling your cock while you slept. By the time he was awake enough to realize someone was sucking his dick, he wasn't able to think clearly enough to put a stop to it if he'd wanted to. Not that he'd ever want to. After all, what was he gonna do, declare a time out? Kind of a moot point, anyhow, because it was all so damn dreamlike that were it not for the sound of the door clicking shut, he'd almost think it hadn't happened. But for the musky scent of aroused woman that lingered on his sheets, there was no evidence of what had taken place. If only he could bottle that aroma for a memento.

He scratched his chest, rubbed the sleep from his face, stretched out his arms, then propped his head on his bent arms, trying to analyze what had happened. The last thing he'd known before going to sleep was that Elise was snoring away on the far side of the bed, fully clothed. After he'd gotten ready for bed, he stripped down like he did every night of his life, and settled under the blankets, respectfully as far away from his unexpected "houseguest" as possible. Hell, he'd even turned his back away from her for good measure.

Next thing he knew he was about to blow his load into her mouth and he sure as hell hadn't instigated that. He hoped Elise had finally realized how irrational she'd been all those years ago—and continued to be. And that she'd decided to make up for lost time the moment that happened.

Of course, now he realized what probably happened is that she was either sleep-fucking—was that a thing?—or she thought she was turning on some other guy. Probably the dickhead in the ten-gallon hat. He wanted to believe it was sleep-fucking. Because surely that would be no different than waking up and walking into the shower or wandering down the street. That shit happened all the time, didn't it? Hell, there was that thing with some sleeping pill that caused people to eat a whole bag of hamburger buns in the middle of the night. So maybe she sleep-sucked, for starters, then sleep-fucked for the grand finale, and then in the morning, she realized who her unwitting partner was and freaked out.

One thing was for sure: she must've freaked out. He chuckled. He could only imagine her this morning upon waking—her instincts would've been like a cat whose tail got caught under a rocker. But then she'd have been conflicted for fear of waking him—the last thing she'd want to do is face the music with him if she was riddled with regrets. He'd have loved to see how she managed to round up her clothes and slip out the door without waking him. She must've been shitting bricks.

He replayed what had happened in his mind, from the minute central command in his brain told him that someone's tongue was stroking his cock, to the moment she insisted that he enter her from behind. Although he regretted that this didn't afford him the chance to put his mouth on hers or to suck on her nipples, although he had at least reached around her to tweak them with his fingers. It had been years since his eyes had feasted on those gorgeous tits, though, so he lamented missing out on the opportunity. And then, of course, he replayed the moment he buried himself deep inside her and stilled himself as his body convulsed in such overwhelming pleasure, he was amazed he didn't shout loud enough to wake the neighbors.

He rolled off the bed and padded to the bathroom. His foot made contact with something other than carpet. He stooped over and picked up a tiny slip of silky black fabric and dangled it above his head as he gave a long, low whistle. Well, if he couldn't package up the smell of sex on his sheets, at least he would be able to pocket the smell of Elise on her panties—slight concession. His eyes scanned the carpet for any other parting gifts, which was when he found the matching silky black push-up bra poking out from beneath the bed. This was good. What better conversation starter with Elise at the rehearsal dinner tonight than the fact that he was carrying her matching bra and panties along as a memento of their hot little session. You never knew if they'd come in handy or not.

Ricardo was waiting for Will in the lobby.

"I'm starving, man. What took you so long?"

Will shrugged. For now, he was going to keep this under his hat. No sense in everyone hearing about this—it would only make Elise more skittish than she already was.

"Just getting a slow start. Where'd you get that?" he asked, pointing at his friend's coffee cup. "I need caffeine something fierce."

Ricardo pointed to a line with easily fifteen people in it. "Let's get to the diner and you'll have all the coffee your heart desires."

Will nodded, then pulled on his hoodie as they left the hotel. Probably far greater chance of avoiding the morning-after interrogations anyhow if he stayed clear of everyone who might have seen him leaving last night with a certain someone dangling over his shoulders.

They walked the two blocks to Grady's Eggs & Pies and settled into a booth in the back of the spacious diner. Will flipped his coffee cup in a less-than-subtle manner to indicate his dire need for java.

The waitress came by and filled it. "What'll it be boys?"

"Western omelet, home fries, and a side of bacon, please." He grinned at the waitress. "And a healthy slice of huckleberry pie."

"At ten in the morning?" Ricardo knit his brow.

"Trust me, the pie's the best part."

His friend nodded. "Great. Gimme one slice huckleberry and the other slice, chocolate cream. And a side of bacon."

The two men laughed.

"Michelle hiding from you today? Or she doesn't want to watch you eat weird shit?"

"She's pretty hung this morning," Ricardo said. "I think all the ladies were pretty shit-faced. Basically, all those shots Jennifer and her girls were doing? It was like a wave at a football game, with a constant passing around and throwing back of shots."

Which made Will happy—the drunker everyone else was, the fewer people might have even noticed what had gone on with him and Elise. And those who noticed may well have forgotten. The only one he needed to worry about was Elise and he was fairly certain she remembered. No doubt to her own chagrin.

"Looks like I was the only one not out of my mind drunk last night," Will said.

Ricardo scratched at his unshaven chin. "Yeah, what was up with you last night? One minute I see you mixing it up with that guy coming on to your old girlfriend, the one you hugged yesterday, and the next you're lugging her ass out of the bar, and we never saw you again. So did you two do it?"

Will felt a rush of heat climb from his chest, along his neck, then across his face. So much for no one noticing. He pursed his lips. "It was nothing. That guy's from my high school and he's an asshole. He was getting handsy with her and she was so drunk I wanted to make sure she was safe from him."

"So you two didn't—" He formed a circle with his thumb and pointer finger of one hand and pressed his pointer finger of his other hand into the circle.

Will shook his head. "What'd you learn that little hand gesture at sixth-grade summer camp?" He rolled his eyes. "Nothing like that. It was all good." There. He didn't lie, but he managed to evade the truth. Perfect.

"All good would mean you got laid. This doesn't sound good at all."

Will frowned. "Did I not already tell you she hates my guts?" Though maybe she still had an affinity for his cock. If only.

"Was just hoping you'd get a little wedding action,

maybe get that ex-girlfriend to realize how much she had a jones for boner. A jonser for your boner." He laughed. "I crack myself up."

Will rolled his eyes. "At least someone does."

The waitress brought their food, and Will wrinkled his brow as he watched his friend crunch bacon into his pies.

Ricardo grinned, chocolate cream pie in his teeth. "What? Everything's better with bacon."

"Even sex?"

Ricardo next scooped a fat forkful of huckleberry pie into his mouth, and chewed, looking away as if lost in thought for a minute. Then he nodded. "Yup. Even sex."

Will's eyes opened wide. "Seriously, I do not want to know what you just remembered in that twisted mind of yours that involved bacon and sex."

His buddy held his hands up in surrender. "You asked. I was only telling you."

"Hey fellas." Will turned to see Jennifer, a posse of bridesmaids in her wake. "I see you needed a pie fix this morning as well?"

"Yeah, well, nothing says hangover cure better than a slice of Grady's finest," Will said as he popped a bite into his mouth.

"Kinda weird alongside eggs, but totally what I need this morning." She massaged her temples.

Will tried to discreetly look past her to the line at the front of the restaurant to see if Elise was with the group. A few of the women—all blond, naturally—had their backs turned to him and so who knew if one of them was her. It's not like he'd been studying her in her newly blond state enough to distinguish her. Though he ought to be able to recognize her from behind... He grinned to himself.

"Something funny?" Jennifer said, lifting a brow.

He shook his thoughts out of his head. "Sorry, got distracted for a second there."

The hostess approached Jennifer. "I've got your table all set up in the back if you want to round up your party."

Jennifer turned around and whistled as though she were calling in a work crew for supper. The whole restaurant stopped and became quiet. Which was right when Elise turned and her eyes locked on Will's. And her face flushed with embarrassment as he held her gaze, hoping to convey something—he didn't have any idea what—to her. Just as quickly, the women all organized to follow Jennifer toward their table, and as they swept past his table, he tried to smile at her, but she turned her head away from him as if he didn't exist.

Well, maybe that little accidental nighttime dalliance only served to make things even harder for him. The good news was Will never met a challenge he didn't rise to, and now that he'd had a taste of the grown-up version of Elise Jackson, he was more determined than ever to go back for seconds.

Chapter Seven

"SO, what was with the intense staring contest going on between you and Will?" Jennifer arched her thumb toward him.

Elise pretended she didn't hear her friend's question as she moved a bite of pie around on her plate with her fork. But she knew Jen wasn't going to settle for a little stonewalling, even of the pie-shifting variety.

"Eh?" her friend tapped her on the shoulder.

"What do you mean?"

Jennifer crossed her arms over her chest. "You can play dumb with me, but you know and I know that I'm not stupid. Something is going on with you two. Can't start a fire without a spark, and unless I've completely lost my intuition, which I can assure you I haven't, I would say there has been some serious smoldering going on. Care to fill me in?"

Elise heaved a sigh. "Seriously, Jen, this is your wedding weekend. You've got your rehearsal dinner tonight, and there's so much last-minute stuff to focus on. You do not need to worry your pretty little head about my nonsense."

Jennifer rested her hand on top of Elise's. "Sweetie, it's not called worrying. It's what we call caring. Besides, I feel responsible, since my act of omission did kind of put you on the spot with Will this weekend."

If only she knew how I put myself *on the spot with my own act of drunken idiocy.*

Elise dismissed that notion with a flick of her hand. "I'm a big girl and I can handle a little awkwardness with Will Montgomery."

Jennifer rubbed her lips together. "So... there's awkward, and then there's awkward," she said. "And a little birdie told me that you were seen exiting the bar slung over the shoulder of a certain tall, dark and handsome ex-boyfriend of yours. Does that fall under the category of vicious rumor or is it possible that actually happened and I missed it?"

Elise rolled her eyes and shook her head. "It's a long story." She sighed, wincing as she tried to figure out what to say. She splayed her hands on the tabletop and leaned slightly toward her friend. "I think by then you and Jamie had already gone back to your room to fuck like rabbits. And I might have been a little drunk—"

"If it's any consolation, we did not fuck like rabbits." She paused half a beat, then held up her finger. "More like bonobo apes." She started laughing at her joke, and Elise playfully punched her in the arm.

"This is not a laughing matter. Do you want to hear this or not?"

Jennifer rested her chin on her hands and leaned in. "You've got some dish for me? Hell to the yeah, I want to hear it!"

"Fine. But you are ridiculously sworn to secrecy. Not even Jamie can know about this. Promise?"

"I swear to you on my dog I won't breathe a word."

Elise frowned. "You don't even own a dog."

"I felt like it was bad juju to swear on, like my grandmother. It was the first thing that came to mind. But really, you know I'm totally good to keep it between us two. Now spill."

"So, I got pretty drunk—as much as I can remember, I did. I was super stressed out about that whole thing yesterday—finding out about Will when he freaking charity-hugged me and all was so not on my to-do list. Maybe I capitulated to peer pressure more than usual and did wayyyy too many shots. I mean, I don't even like tequila, so Lord knows why I did all those shots. But that's water under the bridge." She took a deep breath. "So then, what's that guy's name we went to school with? Tad? Tod? Something like that. The one who wears the cowboy hat. Is he bald maybe? Or he's hiding his prematurely thinning hair? He was getting a bit handsy with me—at least I hear that's the case—and who but Will swoops in all manly and determined and hauls me off like a sack of concrete after threatening bodily harm to Tod/Tad."

Jennifer leaned in even more, her fingers tightly clasped as she latched on to Elise's every word. "So let's cut to the chase. You guys went back and kissed and made up?"

Elise shook her head. "I passed out cold!"

Jennifer sat up. "Wait—I thought this was going to be titillating news that was going to thrill and excite me. You passed out? How boring is that?"

Elise drummed her fingers on the table. Thank God the rest of the bridesmaids were busy chatting with one another. She so didn't want this to be the topic of conversation for the weekend. "But then I woke up some time in the middle of the night. Things get a little sketchy here with my recall. But I think I've pieced together enough of this to generally have my facts straight, so bear with me."

She looked up to search out her waitress for a coffee refill, only to once again make eye contact with Will. Argh. She looked away but her face grew warm, making her seem like a stupid schoolgirl with a crush on the star quarterback.

Only she did *not* have a crush on anyone. It was all a complete misunderstanding. Except that she kind of, sort of wouldn't mind terribly if she could have a little bit of a command performance. She'd forgotten how much she missed sex. Not to mention how much she'd missed sex with Will. Even drunken unprotected mistake sex.

The waitress came over and filled her cup, and Elise continued.

"I guess I got up to pee, and I must've been hot, so I stripped off my clothes, and went back to bed, but I realized there was a man sleeping next to me, and I thought it was Tad/Tod/Ted. And I decided—now bear with me, I think I was still drunk, so I wasn't making good choices—that it would behoove me to have a one-night stand since I hadn't been with anyone in like a lifetime."

"Whoa!"

"Yeah, whoa. But it gets worse."

Jennifer's eyes widened. "How much worse could it get?" She took a swig of her water.

"I went down on him and then had sex with him. And I didn't even think to insist on a condom. And it turned out to be Will."

Jennifer choked on her water. "You gave an accidental blow job to Will? Then had sex with him?"

Elise winced. "Technically it was a deliberate blow job, but it was accidentally done to Will. Ditto for the sex."

"Oh. My. God." Jennifer fanned herself. "I'm speechless. Elise. This is epic." She reached for her friend's hand and clasped them. "You and Will! Together again!"

Slamming her coffee cup down, Elise wiped the air with her hands to erase that whole crazy concept. "Are you insane? I can't be with him! It was all a huge mistake!"

"But it was good, right?"

"I don't know! I mean yes. Or maybe. I was still half drunk. And I thought it was with someone else. So it's hard to gauge."

"All the more reason to give it another go to see for sure."

Elise shook her head wildly. "God, no! I'm going to totally pretend it didn't happen. If anyone asks about whatever happened to me last night, the party line is that I ended up with Tod/Tad/Ted. Got it?"

Jennifer squinted. "But won't Tod/Tad know that's a lie? And even more so, won't Will?"

"Not like Will is going to broadcast it to the world. He's not that kind of guy. And Tod's not invited to the wedding, right? What're the chances I'll even see him again this weekend? It's kind of the perfect excuse."

Jennifer shrugged. "I dunno, Elise. I think this all sounds a little lame. You and Will hooked up! That's great news! Let's celebrate it and repeat it and see if it sticks!"

"Nothing has changed between us. Things happened long ago that proved I couldn't trust him. Why would I ever expect that to change? I am far better off without Will Montgomery in my life."

Jennifer cocked her head, glancing at her friend from the corner of her eyes. "Okay, babe. Just keep telling yourself that. But maybe you should keep in mind that you've got a few more chances for a booty call before the weekend's out."

"Over my cold dead body," Elise said, although if she were honest with herself, she'd admit that she much preferred to be under his warm, live one.

Chapter Eight

THE rehearsal dinner was at a restaurant up in the mountains at the nearby ski resort with a wall of windows that gave a breathtaking view of the surrounding Rockies. It was this sort of thing that made Elise question her decision to move far away from here. Something about Bristol spoke to her despite her leaving and never looking back. Maybe with maturity came perspective. Back then, she was sad and bitter and wanted to distance herself from the scene of her heartbreak. But now she was looking at this place through a different lens.

She'd been working in DC in what felt like a go-nowhere job, spinning her wheels as a legislative assistant and realizing that those jobs all came down to your boss needing to raise money to maintain power. She'd landed there out of college only because a friend had taken on a similar job and suggested she apply; she said she was having fun in DC. At the time it sounded like a nice change of pace, a big, exciting city over the more rural upbringing she'd been used to.

Since she wasn't sure of her career path, she figured she'd try it on for size, only to learn it had very little charm. One thing became clear: she wanted to be a part of change for the better and had no interest in treading water and rarely seeing rewards for her hard work.

During the cocktail hour before the rehearsal dinner,

she'd run into a woman she'd vaguely known in high school—someone who had headed up the conservation club when Elise was a freshman and this woman, Marissa Collier, was a senior. Now Marissa was spearheading efforts to set aside private lands to preserve habitats for the important wildlife that thrived in this wild country and to keep development and energy exploration from encroaching too close to the national park.

"I could use more help," Marissa said as she took a sip of her champagne. "We're working on several large grant applications right now, and I need more help with that plus someone who could be good with fundraising. There are so many untapped financial resources around here—visitors who come to Montana to enjoy this pristine land and want to help preserve it for future generations, for instance. I need someone with ambitious ideas about how to better reach out to these folks and to keep them coming back. The grant writing can be a bit tedious, but honestly being able to identify organizations with shared interests and join forces with them is very rewarding."

"That sounds so interesting," Elise said, taking a sip of her Perrier. After last night, even the lure of champagne held no sway over her. "And the work is all back here in Bristol?"

She nodded. "Yep. I know that's unappealing to some young adults—the idea of getting away from hokey little towns and all. But this place"—she spread her arms out in front of the wall of windows—"I mean, what's not to love?"

Elise knew that was undeniable. The scenic beauty, the clean air, and the lack of traffic were all pretty appealing. Even the tourist crowds held nothing to what she dealt with on her daily commute into DC from Virginia. And she had to basically flee hours away to the Shenandoah Mountains to get her nature fix, whereas right here you could be in the mountains in ten simple minutes. Bristol offered spectacular summers, short but breathtakingly beautiful autumns, cold but activity-filled winters, and wildflower-infused springtimes.

If she moved back here, she'd be closer to Jen and Jamie, which would be nice. Though would that be weird hanging out with the married couple? Maybe she could try to give Tod/Tad/Ted a chance. See what was under that big ole Stetson of his. Speaking of big, though, she'd certainly find herself nowhere near any big ole anything of Will's, which made her a bit wistful all of a sudden. Was it because whatever happened last night stirred up feelings that had never gone away? Or because she hadn't been properly laid in forever? She gave herself a mental growl because it was all a moot point anyhow.

Marissa had plucked a business card from her purse and was handing it to Elise. "Give me a call if you'd like to talk more. I think we could be a great fit."

Elise nodded. "I'd like that. Thanks." She stared out the window as the late afternoon sun burnished the mountains with a warm, salmon-tinged glow. An eagle rode the thermals in the distance. Nearby there were likely bears searching for their next meal among the plentiful berry bushes. And somewhere, a young father was introducing his son to the joys of fly fishing, and a mother was maybe setting up a tent with her girls for a night under the stars. She was only starting to realize that what DC had taught her was that DC wasn't right for her—that this wild, but slightly settled place offered her exactly what she hadn't realized she needed in her life. Maybe it was time she started to think about making some big life changes.

"I'll be in touch for sure. Now, if you'll excuse me, I need to find the ladies' room before we're seated for dinner."

They shook hands and Elise wandered back past the long, polished copper bar, following the signs toward the restrooms. She exited through a fire door down a flight of steps. She opened yet another door and nearly smacked heads with Will.

"Elise." He gave her a hesitant smile.

She nodded back. "Will." She'd hoped to continue in the direction of the bathroom, but he'd planted himself smack in the way of any forward momentum, then rested his palms on her shoulders.

"We should talk," he said, staring into her eyes.

"Look, Will, don't trap me here against my will. I've got mad skills with self-defense, so don't make me use them on you." That was a total lie but it sounded good.

He chuckled. "Bad enough you slapped me. Now you're going to beat up the best man? I don't think Jamie and Jennifer would appreciate that."

"Yeah, well."

"Yeah, well, you would do yourself a favor if you stopped hiding behind ancient biases and instead maybe deal with the here and now of things. You know, new information and all."

"Ummm, what new information?"

He squinted at her. "You're going to play that game with me?"

"I have no idea what you're talking about."

He shook his head. "Even after I defended your honor with that stupid prick, Tad."

"Tod." She took a deep breath. "Or maybe it's Ted. It could be Tad."

"Let's agree it's 'Turd' and call it a day."

Despite herself, she broke into a smile.

"I can't stop thinking about last night, Elise." He'd slid

his hand from her shoulder to clasp her hand.

"I don't know what you're talking about." Oh, she was so going to rot in hell for that lie. But maybe she could convince him it was all in his head?

"Look, Elise, you can pretend all you want, but you know and I know what happened between us last night was real."

She furrowed her brow. "Maybe you're mistaking me for someone else?"

"Oh, you think so, do you?" He reached into his pocket and pulled out something. "I see your taste in panties has grown more sophisticated." He pressed the delicate black lace beneath his nose. "Last I recall you were all about the 'days of the week' undies."

She tried to grab the panties from his hand, but he pulled away too quickly, tucking them into the breast pocket of his suit coat. He shrugged. "Tut-tut, Elise," he said, shaking his head. "You wouldn't want to deprive a man of the next best thing if he can't have his own nose right *there*." He looked down toward her crotch.

She rolled her eyes. "Fat chance."

He squinted. "It's my fault for not having returned the favor, you know." He winked at her and gave her a little smack on the bottom. "It's just that I pretty much lost my mind with that dirty little mouth of yours wrapped around my cock. I truly thought I was dreaming for the first few minutes. And then when you asked me to slide into you from behind…" He clutched at his heart as if he were having a heart attack. "Well, what's a gentleman to do but please the lady as she requested?"

Crap. It looked like there was no mistaking what exactly happened last night after all.

"Look, don't get your hopes up. I thought you were

him."

"Him who?"

"That guy. Tod. Tad. Whatever."

"Turd?"

"Yeah, him."

"So you thought you were having sex with a guy named Turd?"

She rolled her eyes and shook her head. "Of course not. The Turd part is new."

"Oh, so it was before we deemed him Turd, so that makes it okay?"

"Yes! I mean no! I mean, it's none of your business."

"The guy was groping all over you and you were clearly too drunk to have that happening to you."

"Oh, so you took it upon yourself to be my savior?"

"I sure as hell didn't see anyone else stepping up to the plate."

"Maybe because I didn't need to be saved."

"So, you'd have been totally fine with going home in a drunken stupor with a guy who respected you so little that he was sticking his hands all over your body at a bar? I don't buy it."

She crossed her arms and pursed her lips. "Well… whatever." *Good comeback, Elise.*

"Look, Elise. Feel free to be the last one to get the memo that you and I have got unfinished business to attend to." He pointed at her and then at himself. "What happened last night between the two of us is proof of that. You can deny it all you want, but you're only failing yourself by not following your own instincts."

She glared at him. "Newsflash: been there, done that, still licking my wounds."

She could see Will was getting frustrated by the very

clench of his jaw. And a little part of her understood that perhaps she was being irrational about things, but how could she not be?

He held up his hands. "I give up. Ball's in your court. If all I take away from this is this memento"—he pulled out her panties and slid them beneath his nose again—"well, then I guess I'll have to settle for what you'll give me." With that, he slipped through the door and back up the steps, leaving Elise to be the one to grind her teeth in frustration. Or was it confusion?

Chapter Nine

WHY Will thought he could get through to Elise right now would have to remain a mystery. It was obvious she was either freaked out by what happened—or by how her body responded to it—or she was simply in complete denial. There was little he could do on his end to try to clear things up. At this point, he was at the mercy of divine intervention.

When he got back up to the main floor of the restaurant, everyone was already seated for the dinner service. He worked his way toward the front of the dining room to the table reserved for the wedding party and took a seat. He couldn't help but grin when Elise arrived back at the table five minutes later to find the only remaining seat was immediately to his left.

Paging divine intervention, please pick up on line one…

He decided to take this as a sign.

Seated to his right was Red, the little gal who so brazenly came on to him at the bar last night. Perhaps he could milk this to his advantage.

"Sammi," he said, reaching for her hand and kissing the back of it. "So lovely to get to share your charming company tonight." He knew damn well that Elise would have one ear to his conversation throughout dinner and hoped she'd noticed that gesture too.

"You don't know the half of it!" Sammi quickly wrapped the fingers of her just-kissed hand around his bicep, like she was measuring the diameter with the span of her hand. Weird. "Oooh, so strong and brawny."

Okay then, he'd yet to have anyone make color commentary on his body like this before. Maybe this was what women felt like when construction workers catcalled them: shamelessly objectified. Of course, he was a guy, so feeling objectified wasn't exactly a bad thing—more like a big fat ego boost.

Under other circumstances, he'd be on it in a heartbeat—who wouldn't want a cute chick coming on hard like that? But he only wanted to daunt Elise a bit, not encourage Sammi's come-ons much. This could be trickier than he expected, striking a balance between the two. After all, he knew it would make Elise a little crazy having to listen to verbal foreplay between him and Red. But he needed to make sure it stopped there and Red didn't get any ideas that something would come of it.

Just as the entrée was served, Will caught wind of the conversation Elise was having with Candy Kettering, the brunette she was with for the charity hugs—which seemed like it had happened weeks earlier but was only two days ago.

"Is it true that you hooked up with that guy who was all over you at the bachelorette party? The one with the cowboy hat?"

Elise gave Candy a coy wink. "Oh my God, Candy. It was amazing. I've never had, like, anonymous-stranger sex in the dark before, but it was so alluring and, well, sexy. Who knew he could be so hot?"

Will saw her glance at him from the corner of her eyes and he just rolled his. If she wanted to play this game, then fine. He wasn't going to lose sleep over it.

"Obviously I'm no expert, but let's say that quasi-anonymous sex in the dark is simply not to be missed. Not to get too granular, but trust me, you have to try it at least once in your life. It revs up your awareness and it's as if all of your senses are so heightened. Know what I mean?"

He leaned over to join in the conversation. "I totally know what you're talking about. Funny, I had the very same experience the other night, and holy shit, when you're sound asleep in the dark and the next thing you know someone is making love to you like she means it, and you know she's as turned on as you are, well, nothing can compare."

Elise's eyes widened like a lemur's. And if those eyes could talk, they would be saying, "Shut the ever-loving fuck up and don't tell people that you and I had sex together!" Not that he was planning to. But oh, how fun it was to flip this on her head.

Sammi raised her hand to join in the conversation. "Is this like, a thing, here in Bristol? Anonymous late-night sex? 'Cause I'd love to know where to sign up for that."

"Uh, surely you're well acquainted with Tinder," Elise said with a smirk.

He leaned in to whisper into Elise's ear. "Or you could find the person you're meant to make love with and let bygones be bygones and get on with the fun stuff. Because we both know how much you enjoyed yourself."

Elise choked on her water. Jesus, the man knew how to get her hot and bothered. Because yeah, she had indeed enjoyed herself. And she couldn't help but yearn for a command performance, one where she'd have better command of her senses, considering she was still a bit drunk last time around. Over the past day, she kept having little snippets of recall—tiny raindrops of clarity in her alcohol-tainted memories that landed in her mind and spread like drops of gasoline in a puddle, till she couldn't compartmentalize the truth anymore: she'd never truly let go of Will Montgomery. Now that she'd had a taste of him, she didn't know how to walk away from him yet again.

After dinner came the requisite speeches. At this point, she was clock-watching to get out of here and far, far away from the temptation seated to her right. She just needed to get through the next twenty or so minutes of premarital platitudes and she'd be good to go.

First, Jennifer and Jamie stood up and clinked their glasses to get everyone's attention.

"Jamie and I are so very grateful that you all chose to share this special occasion with us." Jen reached over and clasped her fiancé's hand. "Each and every one of you has had an important influence in our lives, and we would have been so heartbroken to have missed out on having any of you here—"

Jamie winked at their friends gathered around them. "Which was why Jen and I decided to lie and not even tell our maid of honor and best man that the other would be in the wedding party—we knew for them it would be a deal breaker, after their unpleasant breakup years ago. But what kind of wedding would this be without the two of them here? So, props to Elise and Will for setting aside their differences for the greater good!"

They both lifted their glasses in the air as the guests all toasted them. And while Elise bore a somewhat pinched expression on her face, Will broke into laughter and stood up.

"Well, well, well. Look who had the last laugh. I can't say that I'm disappointed, though. I'd not have missed this weekend for the world, and to be honest, having Elise here would have only been added incentive to attend. As they say, time heals old wounds, and here's hoping whatever scar tissue I might have left behind is pretty much invisible by now." He turned to Elise. "Elise—it wouldn't be the same without you here, so I'm glad you didn't turn tail and run the minute you saw me back in town."

Elise was filled hot shame at being singled out as the center of attention like this. It wasn't even her special weekend—why then did they have to draw attention to her? Now everyone was going to start probing to find out all the dirty details, which she had zero interest in rehashing at this point. Over the next few minutes, while others stood up to speak, Elise dwelled on this. And the more she focused on it, the more anxious she became. The more anxious she became, the more shallow her breathing became, and before she knew it, she felt light-headed.

She turned to Candy. "I feel wooz—" But she never got out the "y" before she started to fall toward Will, who amazingly caught her before she was able to hit the floor.

She had no idea how much time had passed, but all she knew was that she was looking up from what seemed to be Will's lap into his marine-blue eyes, concern knitting his brow, as he scraped his fingers through her hair and gently called out her name.

Whoa. She must've been dreaming.

Chapter Ten

ELISE could vaguely hear Jennifer urging Will to take her back to his room, but oh, man, she knew even in her altered state that was an awful idea. Look what happened last time she was hauled off to his hotel room against her will! She tried to voice her objections, but speaking seemed too cumbersome. It felt easier to let Will comb through her hair with his fingers, scratching her scalp in the way she always used to love.

Apparently, the wife of someone at the rehearsal dinner was a doctor who looked her over and thought the best course of action would be to find her somewhere to lie down. She didn't think Elise was in any danger. Except Elise knew she'd be in imminent danger—of falling even more for Will—if she actually went back to his room.

It took both Will and Jamie to hoist Elise up to a standing position.

"Can someone give you two a ride back to the hotel?" Jen said.

"No worries—you guys stay here. There's an Uber on the way and I've got everything under control."

It was slight consolation that Will hadn't flung her over his shoulder again at least. Some guy named Ricardo helped Will get her down to the curb where the Uber was waiting for them.

"Dude, good luck," he said. "Maybe you can have more

success this time around than you did last night."

Huh. Elise was lucid enough to get what he was saying. So this guy didn't know what had happened between Will and her last night? He didn't go boasting to all of his peeps about doing her? How very unguy-like of him. Make that how gentlemanly of him. Strange how Will didn't cease to surprise her.

Once in the car, Elise tried to raise her objections. "I'm fine going back to my room." She held her hand up in protest. "In fact, you can tell the driver to wait and take you back to the party. No sense in both of us missing out on the fun."

It fleetingly crossed her mind that they could make their own fun, but she knew better than that.

"Please, Elise. I'm not going to leave you alone twenty minutes after you passed out. And if you think I would, you don't know me at all."

Which was the problem, wasn't it? She didn't know him. Or she thought she knew him and didn't. Even when she knew him, she didn't know him. And now she couldn't figure out who exactly Will Montgomery was: friend or foe? Potential lover, or betrayer? The only thing she knew for sure right now was that he was a well-endowed ex who, she discovered, had learned a lot of tricks in bed in the intervening years that only served to please her. And that, without a doubt, was hard to dismiss.

Will would not take no for an answer and insisted on walking Elise through the hotel lobby, into the elevator, and down the long corridor to his room with his arm snaked around her midsection supporting her.

He pressed the keycard to the lock and opened the door, then walked her to the bed where they stopped. She closed her eyes against the memories flooding back from the night before, the slow glide as Will slid into her slick center, that moment when they both stilled as their bodies climaxed in unison. Wowza. She was in deep.

"Okay, so have a seat and I'll help you slip off your shoes," he said, helping her settle onto the bed. He reached past her to prop up the pillows so she could at least sit up, and he bent down to remove her shoes, lifting her feet onto the bed. "Blanket on or off?"

She shrugged.

"Okay, I'll take that to mean on." He shifted the blanket so that it draped over her up to her midsection, then grabbed the remote control from the nightstand. "Movie okay?"

She shrugged.

"You're just full of opinions tonight, aren't you?"

"Do I have a choice in the matter?"

"On having an opinion? I would say so."

"On being here at all."

It was his turn to shrug. "Look, Elise. I've taken on the responsibility of making sure that you're okay and I'm going to fulfill that responsibility. You passed out at the rehearsal dinner. I'm not going to leave you alone in your room!"

She shook her head. "Fine. Movie."

"Any particular genre?"

"How about one involving mass destruction. End of the world would be a good start."

"You sure are cheerful." He aimed the remote at the television and pulled up the menu. "I'll take that to mean you'd like to watch a romantic comedy."

At least he didn't unilaterally decide to switch on porn.

After selecting a film, he went to the minibar and grabbed a beer for himself and a bottle of water for her. He even rifled through the tea selection and heated up hot water to make her some herbal tea.

"Figured you probably weren't hydrated enough back at the restaurant, so here, drink up."

He plopped down on the other side of the bed as the movie started to play.

It was so weird, the two of them, like old times, watching a movie together as if years hadn't passed. As if hurt and betrayal hadn't gotten in the way of things the way it had.

They watched the film in silence for a while. When the inevitable scene came on in which there was a misunderstanding and one partner walked away from the other, Elise had to speak up.

"Can I ask you something?"

Will had slunk down in the bed and was now lying sideways facing Elise. "Fire away."

"Why did you do it?"

"Make you come here tonight?"

She shook her head. "No, dummy. It. Why did you do *it*? Why would you have betrayed me and given up what we had together like you did?"

Will rolled his eyes. "We've been over this so many times, Elise. I didn't betray you. You chose to think that I did."

"Then what happened? Where'd you go? Why were you so secretive?"

"Because it would have betrayed someone's confidence, that's why." He reached out for her hand and laced his fingers through hers. "I asked you then and I'll ask again for you to trust me and know that I am not and was never

65

the bad guy you made me out to be."

"How can I know that?"

"I think the bigger question is how could you not know that?"

He stroked along the top of her hand with his thumb.

It all felt so familiar and… good. And yet, how could something so wrong feel so right?

She turned so she was lying on the bed facing him. She reached out and traced along his goatee. "Did I tell you I like how this looks?"

He smiled. "I aim to please."

She couldn't help but think how it would feel against her mouth, or better yet sliding along other exposed parts of her body.

"Speaking of pleasing," he continued, "I'm not sure if I should be insulted that you had so much fun last night but only because you didn't know it was me you were with."

She groaned. "I'm not sure if I'm ready to talk about that." She pursed her lips. "I'm not sure I'll ever be ready to talk about that."

"Are you ashamed that you did what you did and didn't care that it was a random fling?" He traced his finger along her mouth. "Because I find that's pretty damn sexy. A woman confident in her sexuality and willing to take charge is pretty hot if you ask me."

Elise's face heated for what seemed like the hundredth time this weekend. "You don't think it was a little, oh, slutty of me?"

He shook his head. "If this was a regular habit of yours, I might think you'd want to reconsider your actions. But under the circumstances, no. And being on the receiving end of it, hell no!"

"It's only that I hadn't been with anyone in forever,"

she said. "I thought maybe it would all atrophy if I didn't do something sometime soon." She pointed toward her crotch. "And here I found myself in bed with a naked man, and it seemed so salacious, so subversive, so not something I'd do—it felt right."

"It felt even more right to me," he said and leaned in, this time using his tongue to trace along her lips. "Like right enough to demand a command performance, even."

He licked along the seam of her lips and coaxed them open where his tongue met hers and began the age-old mating dance as each explored the other's mouths, teeth, tongues, lips.

She let out a groan.

Will paused for a moment, lifting her chin with his fingertip as their eyes locked. "You okay with this?"

Elise was more okay with this than she ought to be, but the idea of not following through on this right now seemed like complete folly. She nodded and reached out to unbutton his shirt, sending a message that was loud and clear.

Will tugged down the thin straps of her cocktail dress and reached behind to unzip it, shimmying it down her body, then shaking his arms out of his shirt and tossing it aside.

He moved over top of her, angling his mouth on hers. She gasped in pleasure at the feel of his bare chest pressed to her breasts. For the first time, clearheaded and with unequivocal intent, she was moving forward with this plan, unconcerned with the outcome. It felt right, and that was all that mattered right now.

Will's hands skimmed along her sides, from the underside of her arms down along her hips. As his fingers explored her body, his thumbs hooked into her panties and easily tugged them down so that his fingers could move to her already slick center. They moaned into one another's mouths as they both enjoyed the sensation of his fingers gliding through her wetness.

"God, Elise. I can't tell you how turned on I am right now," he said as he began to shift his body down, his mouth kissing and licking a path first to one nipple and then the other, which he suckled to a tight, hard tip. Elise dragged her nails through his hair as he moved down more, swirling his tongue in her belly button, then on a trail to the neatly trimmed patch of hair at her pubic bone. She didn't think it was necessary to say that she was likely even more turned on than he was, especially after that first long stroke of his tongue, starting at her swollen clit and continuing on along the length of her lips. She thrust her hips toward him and relished the added sensation of his well-groomed beard trailing behind with each stroke of his tongue. As he inserted first one, then another finger inside her, coating his fingers with her juices, she thought she'd go mad with pleasure. As the pace of her breathing accelerated and the tingling edge of a climax began to spread throughout her pelvis, she pressed his head toward her throbbing clit, desperate for him to tip her over, and his masterful mouth complied, alternately circling her clit with his tongue and sucking with his lips.

"Oh, fuck, Will, right there, now." Her voice was pleading and breathy, and she could no longer control the pace of her thrusting hips, and then her control shattered as his tongue pressed to her clit, her pussy spasming around his fingers and mouth as her orgasm overtook her.

Elise could still feel the faint pulse of her fading climax when she looked up to see Will on his knees, unbuttoning his suit pants and skimming them over his hips, along with his boxer briefs. His huge erection jutted from his body, primed and ready. He locked eyes with her and she nodded.

"What are you waiting for?" she said as she spread her legs wide and pulled him down on top of her body. "Get over here."

Their mouths met again and she dragged her tongue around his lips and mouth, lapping up her own juices from his beard as he notched the swollen tip of his cock at the entrance. "You sure about this, babe?" He arched his brow, his soulful blue eyes imploring.

"I couldn't be any more certain. But hurry. I want to feel your hard cock deep inside me."

That was all the invitation he needed as he thrust in deep, pressing and holding his cock inside her wet depths as his tongue invaded her mouth.

"You are such a tease, Will Montgomery." She grabbed her thighs and spread her legs even farther. "Show me what you've got."

"Oh yeah," he groaned. "Your wish is my command."

With that, he withdrew his dick, then quickly pumped hard into her, dipping his head down to capture a nipple in his mouth as his hips continued their thrusting momentum.

"God, I wish I could have your mouth on me while your cock fucked me," Elise said, feeling herself inching toward the cliff yet again. "I'm close, Will. I want to come on you as you spill yourself into me."

Quickening his pace, he thrust so hard he shifted her body up the bed, her head against the headboard. He pounded into her once, twice, three times and stilled deep inside her, where she could feel wave after wave of come filling her up. It was the most amazing sexual encounter she'd ever experienced, so close to this man she'd once loved so deeply and for whom she couldn't deny her intense and unresolved feelings.

Will's breathing slowed and he leaned down to press a

kiss on Elise's forehead. "That, my dear, was unforgettable."

"Right back atcha," she said, pulling him toward her as they kissed and drifted off to sleep. Un-fucking-forgettable, indeed.

Chapter Eleven

WILL had to pinch himself he was so stoked. In a million years he could never have imagined he and Elise reuniting on any level, let alone getting naked. Of course, he had no idea where this would lead. Hell, he didn't even know where she lived. For all he knew she lived clear across the country, which would suck. Although, he'd think long and hard about following her if he truly thought the two of them could have a chance at something lasting. But these were early days, so he didn't want to get too far ahead of himself.

Elise was sound asleep, curled up to his back, and the temptation was too great to resist, so he reached around and began to play with her nipples. She stirred, pressing her backside up to his groin. He took that as a yes and reached a hand down to slide his fingers along the seam of her pussy, stroking slowly and gently.

She turned her head toward him and he leaned forward to kiss her.

"I can't get over how much I like this little beard you've got going," she said, stroking her hand along his chin. "Although I like even better what you're doing with those busy hands of yours."

"It's nothing compared to how much I love the feeling of my fingers slicking through your wet pussy," he said, nuzzling along her neck as he flipped her around so they were facing one another. He dipped his fingers into her juices and ran them around one nipple, then the other, watching as they tightened at his touch.

"So how do you feel about this?" she pushed him onto his back and climbed on top of him, straddling him, then stroked his hardening cock along her wetness, eliciting a groan from him.

"Put it in and ride me, baby." She was driving him mad with pleasure as she positioned him at her entrance then slid herself down his cock. When he was all the way seated in, she began to grind her hips in a tight, circular motion. He reached up to play with her swollen nipples as she lifted herself off of his cock and slid herself back down again and again.

His mind was lost in the feel of her warm, wet body pulling in his dick.

"Would you mind if we skipped the wedding tomorrow and did this all day instead?"

"As long as you promise to rub that goatee on me again, I think that could be arranged."

She leaned forward, and Will stared at her gorgeous tits as they bounced to the rhythm of her thrusting hips. Life could not get any better than this. He caught a nipple in his mouth and sucked hard, alternately nipping with his teeth, and Elise picked up the pace. He loved seeing a woman own her pleasure like this, and he took a moment to relish watching her work herself toward climax. He encouraged her as she began to moan.

"That's it, baby, ride my cock till your hot pussy clenches around me. Pull the come out of me."

Elise ground her hips hard onto Will, screaming out his name as the flood of her juices bathed his cock. When she stopped shaking, he flipped her onto her back, hooking his arms behind her knees and driving his swollen cock into her slickness, till his balls tightened and his semen surged into her, his body jerking with the intensity of the climax. He collapsed on top of her, his heart racing, his breathing labored.

"Jesus," he said, leaning over to kiss her softly. "You, my dear, are going to be the death of me."

Will startled from a deep sleep when someone began pounding on his door. He hopped out of bed to find out what was going on.

He grabbed a towel off the dresser and slung it around his hips, then opened the door to find a drunk Sammi, her eyes rolling back in her head as she wobbled on her too-high heels.

"Hey there, sexy," she said, pressing a pointer finger into his solar plexus and twirling it around. "I told you I'd come over after the dinner. I figured by now you've gotten rid of Elise, so you and I can have a little play session? I'll show you mine if you show me yours." She licked her lips, which she probably thought looked sexy but in all honesty looked demented.

Will scrubbed his face with his hands. "Um, this is a bad time. We can talk later, 'kay?"

"It's okay. I don't want to talk. I want to fuck."

His eyes bulged open. "Look. You need to leave. I don't want you to get the idea that's going to happen. So, please, do us both a favor and go back to your room and get some sleep."

She tugged on his towel, pulling it off. "But I want to sleep with Y-O-U!" She poked at his bare chest again as she stared at his cock.

Will stood there, slightly in shock as she'd stripped off the only thing keeping him from being exposed to whoever was walking down the hallway.

"Seriously, Sammi."

"Uh, no. It's okay." He heard a voice from behind him. He turned to see Elise, dressed, her shoes dangling from her fingers. Shit. "He's all yours. Once a cheater, always a cheater. I don't know why I thought anything different."

With that, she pushed her way past his naked body, past the drunken poseur trying to get at his body, and he wasn't even able to run after her since Sammi had a death grip on his towel.

Well, crap. Somehow he knew this had all been too good to be true.

Chapter Twelve

ELISE must've finally drifted off to sleep after crying for what seemed like hours. Only to be awoken by the incessant buzzing of her phone sometime around dawn. The good news was that it couldn't be Will calling her—he didn't know her number, nor did he know her hotel room. So at least she was safe from having to deal with him for the time being— she was too damn angry to even know what she'd say to the little shit. She fumbled around on the nightstand till she finally found the thing and answered it.

"Elise—I need your help! Now! There's a tear in my wedding gown and I have to get it to the seamstress, and I'm supposed to be going to get my hair and makeup done. I trust you with your life to get this thing to her and back in one piece. Promise you'll not let the gown out of your sight, okay?"

"Oh, shoot. Jen. What the hell? Of course I'll do that for you." What a godsend—a mission that would distract her from the burning desire to curl up in a ball and sob for the next several hours. "Just text me where I'm supposed to go and I'll meet you in the lobby in five minutes to get the gown from you."

She hopped out of bed and quickly brushed her teeth and washed her face. Her eyes were bloodshot and swollen from crying. She grabbed two cans of cold beer from the minifridge and stuck one over each eye to diminish the puffiness a bit before she went out in public. The last thing she needed was to have people asking what she'd been crying about. Meanwhile, now it looked like hair and makeup would have to take second fiddle to gown repair today, which was a bummer since she needed it more than ever. She'd have to make do and hope she had enough concealer to hide the black rings under her eyes from lack of sleep and too many tears. Worst case with her hair, she could put some soft curls in it and call it a day.

She pulled on a pair of shorts and a tank top—still missing her favorite bra, dammit. If she ever spoke to Will again, she would damn sure reclaim her missing underwear. But that was a big if.

Sliding into a pair of flip-flops, she raced down the hall and impatiently pushed the elevator button repeatedly till the doors opened up. She stepped into the car only to come face-to-face with Will standing there, his hair damp, a pair of sweaty running shorts clinging to his hips. Oh, and no shirt. Her breath hitched in her throat despite herself. Yowza. His chest. It looked so, well, delicious.

She wasn't supposed to have those thoughts about him after what happened last night, dammit! And yet she couldn't look at those well-defined pecs and his tight, sculpted abs without thinking about clutching them as she rode his cock. Was it only hours ago? She made the mistake of avoiding his gaze by glancing downward, where her eyes landed on that glorious zone along the lowered waistband of his shorts. He practically had a welcome mat dangling from his pelvis. Those glorious sex lines of his were cut like gleaming diamonds.

Come to mama.

Not.

Be strong, Elise. Have more self-respect. You do not want to associate with this player who is ready and willing to hook up with anyone at the drop of a hat.

Okay, so instead of staring at that sexy V, her eyes shifted to his happy trail. Which she had licked her tongue along at some point this weekend. Crap. This was not going well at all. It was like she was replaying the "best of" moments with the guy when she needed to remain angry with him. She glanced up to notice that he caught her staring. There.

"Can I help you find something?"

Why yes, as a matter of fact, you can. It's lurking right beneath that waistband.

He stretched his arms and rubbed his hands along his belly. She envied his ability to do that while she stood there and tried not to stare at those lucky, lucky hands.

"Nope, all good." She plastered on one of those fake smiles you give to panhandlers you don't want to engage in conversation with when you pass them on the sidewalk.

"So I don't suppose you've got any interest in discussing what happened last night?"

She shook her head. "Nope. We're good. It was the reminder I needed, thanks." She glanced at her watch to avoid looking at any more of his body parts. "You're out awfully early." She hoped that meant he hadn't allowed Sammi to stick around, but then again, he could easily have done so and sent her packing after the deed was finished.

"Had a hard time sleeping," he said, rubbing that sexy goatee with his hand. Oh God. Now she couldn't stop thinking about that soft goatee rubbing along her private parts. Before last night, she definitely had never felt facial hair *there*. Oh Lord, she was hot and no doubt flushed. This was not good. "Took a run to clear my mind. Went back to my room but realized I had to get something from the car before I showered." He tried to make eye contact but she refused to engage. "You're out awfully early as well."

She shrugged. "Wedding gown crisis. Maid of honor to the rescue."

He nodded. "This is why you pick someone reliable like you for the job—glad Jen knew she could count on you, Elise."

"Yep, that's me. Good ole reliable Elise."

The elevator stopped at the first floor and the doors glided open. She slipped out, proud of herself for not looking back even once.

"Guess I'll see you tonight at the wedding."

"Yup."

And despite what had happened last night, it was like a punch to the gut, knowing that tonight would be it; then no more Will Montgomery for good this time. If only she'd have been a better judge of character.

Elise entered an address into her Waze app and found herself on the outskirts of town at a cute little bungalow set among lodge pines, with wildflowers punctuating the field in front of the home.

She collected up the huge bag containing the wedding gown and ever so gingerly carried it to the front door. A calico cat made a figure eight around her ankles as she rang the doorbell, and a small dog yipped and yapped at the door awaiting its chance to greet her.

When the door opened, Elise was stunned to see none other than Shannon Cadbury—the girl who ruined her high school love affair—standing there, ready to take the package from her arms.

Elise opened her mouth to say something but nothing came out.

"Well, if it isn't Elise Jackson," Shannon said, ushering her into the house.

"I'm so sorry to be here so early, but Jennifer was freaking out and, well, it's her wedding day and all, so, well, here I am." She gave her a tepid smile. "It's, uh, nice to see you. I had no idea you were Jennifer's seamstress."

Shannon looked good—her blond hair had been straightened, and she'd lost a little of the baby fat she'd carried through high school. A glance down showed she was married as well. Huh. Clearly, life was agreeing with her. Elise didn't know whether to be glad for her or hate her after what she'd done.

"Come on in. Let's get you a cup of coffee while you wait."

Elise held up her hands. "Oh, I wasn't planning to wait. I thought I'd come back by—"

She'd planned to drive about two hundred yards away, pull off the road, and read a book. Last thing she wanted to do was sit here and make small talk with the likes of Shannon Cadbury.

"Don't be silly," Shannon said. "It'll be nice to have the company, plus I can show you the work as I go and you can give it your stamp of approval. Oh and here." She grabbed a platter on the counter. "I made some muffins last night for breakfast so you won't go hungry."

Elise scrunched up her nose. Ugh, talk about awkward. But no way to back out of it.

She shrugged. "Sure, thanks."

"First follow me." Shannon led her down a hallway to a large sewing room with gowns hanging along one wall, and a case displaying wedding gown-related notions along another. There were veils suspended from the ceiling, and a rack of various shrugs and capes to wear over the gowns.

"You have quite the setup here. I had no idea you were a talented seamstress."

Shannon smiled. "Me neither. I always knew how to sew, even made most of my own clothes growing up."

"You did?"

"Yep. Sorta had no choice under the circumstances."

Elise hated to ask about circumstances, so she let it slide.

"It wasn't till I got married that I learned to apply my skills to this type of work by apprenticing with my mother-in-law, who's been doing this for years. Bit by bit, I've taken over more of her clients since she's getting ready to retire. In fact, this gown is one she did the alterations on, but she wasn't able to help out this morning, so she asked me to take it on. I was happy to do that because I remember Jennifer from high school."

Gulp. Which means she probably remembers what a shrieking shrew I was after prom. Not my most shining of moments.

All of a sudden, high school seemed so damn long ago and the issues of childhood—because it essentially was still childhood—seemed so frivolous now.

Shannon poured some coffee for Elise and handed her a muffin on a plate, then settled in at a sewing table to get to work.

She held up the gown, inspecting the damage. "Oh, this isn't bad, just some beading that needs to be sewn down again. I can fix this in no time. I was worried it was going to be much more involved."

"Maybe I'll make it back for the glam squad afterward."

Shannon rolled her eyes. "Not that you ever needed a

glam squad. You were always so beautiful."

The heat rose in Elise's face. "Oh, stop. I was a geeky teenager trying to get by like everyone else."

"About as 'geeky'"—she made air quotes with her fingers—"as what's her name, married to Prince William? Duchess Kate?"

Elise spluttered out a laugh. She'd never been compared to exquisite royalty before. "You flatter me far too much." She had to change the subject. Being the object of such undeserved compliments was embarrassing. "So, you're married now?"

Shannon nodded. "Got married two years ago. I wish you could meet Kevin, but he's a firefighter and he's on duty today."

"That's too bad. I'd love to meet him." She smiled, this time a genuine one. "You've sure been busy since graduating from high school."

"What about you—what've you been up to?"

Elise shrugged. "I went to State, then ended up on the East Coast. I work in Washington. My job's okay, but I don't feel particularly passionate about it. In fact, coming back here has made me feel a little homesick for this place."

Shannon's face brightened up. "You thinking about moving back here?"

"Honestly it hadn't crossed my mind until I had a conversation with someone last night who said she was looking for help working in conservation. It's piqued my curiosity a bit, so I'm starting to noodle on rethinking some things."

"Speaking of rethinking things—did you and Will ever make up after you had that spectacular fight after prom?"

Huh. Weird that she'd bring that whole thing up, being that it was due to her, uh, indiscretion.

Elise shook her head. "That just wasn't meant to be."

Shannon threaded a needle and began tacking down the strand of beads that had loosened. "You know, I don't know that I'd have made it out of that year without the kindness of Will Montgomery," she said, her gaze fixed on securing the tiny beads to the delicate fabric. "That night, the boy I'd gone to prom with assaulted me. I was outside crying behind the huge barn when Will came around the corner because he heard my sobs. I was absolutely terrified. Will took my hand and convinced me to go sit with him in his car till I could calm down and decide what to do."

Elise stopped midchew as Shannon confessed her story. "What did you do?"

"You see, I'd asked a boy from my church to be my date. Nobody from our school would've gone with me. I was in such a bad place—my parents were in the process of splitting up and I looked to boys to fill the void in my life. I know the kids had their cruel nicknames for me—everyone thought I was such a slutty girl. But I was such a lonely girl. I wanted to fit in, but I didn't know how. My mom persuaded me to ask this boy from church to go to the prom with me. It was the biggest mistake of my life."

She got up and walked over to her coffee cup—far away from the wedding gown—and took a sip, then returned to her work.

"We had been in a youth group together. His father was the minister at the church. What could go wrong, right?" She grimaced. "At first things were fine, but then he'd snuck in a flask of whiskey and proceeded to get drunk and told me it was time to leave. I didn't want to go, but what was I to do? He was my ride. But I also didn't want him to drive—he was in no shape to be behind the wheel. Still, he ordered me to get into the car and I was a stupid girl. I had no experience with boys, and I didn't know how to respond to his bossiness. All I knew was I wanted to go home.

"So, I got in the car and he locked the doors and proceeded to climb on top of me. It all happened so fast. He shoved up the pretty dress I'd made just for the occasion and ripped my underwear and forced his hands into me so hard he drew blood. I begged him to stop and he kept telling me how lucky I was and how he knew I really wanted it. I was so frightened. Finally I was able to reach over and grab for the door handle, and thank God the lock opened when I pulled the handle and fell out of the car. My dress was covered in mud and there were bloodstains around the crotch, but I got up and ran as fast as my legs would carry me till he was out of sight. That's when I was at the back side of the barn, crying and gasping for air, and Will came up to me."

"What happened to your date?"

"I heard a car peel out of there and assumed—hoped—it was him. I wasn't sure. I was just so grateful I got away from him."

"So then what?"

"Will tried to persuade me to go to the police, but I couldn't do that. It was my church. My mother would have been devastated if I made a big deal about this. Think about it—the minister's son? No one would have believed me, anyhow. So I kept quiet. And I begged Will to keep quiet as well. The last thing I needed was everyone mocking me and teasing me mercilessly about this.

"Will took care of me, held me tight, and promised me he'd make sure I was safe. And he swore his complete confidence, that he'd never breathe anything to a soul. After that I was in such a state of despair, I thought about killing myself. I was so alone and lonely and felt so rejected. Will was the only one who treated me with respect and dignity. And had he not done so, they'd likely have found me at the bottom of a cliff in a heap. I was that down in the dumps. For a long time after that, I kept to myself. I was afraid of my own shadow and stayed away from everyone. It took a long time for me to be able to stop living fearfully."

"How'd you manage that?"

"I met Kevin at a friend's Christmas party. We started out real slowly. I even explained to him what had happened to me—talk about a real buzzkill on a first date, right? So he encouraged me to enroll in a self-defense class that they were offering at the police academy. That gave me the confidence to take care of myself, to not let someone take advantage of me. It was like peeling off a rain-drenched overcoat. I started to feel so light and free. But honestly I'd never have even gotten there were it not for Will. I never did understand why you let go of someone so sweet and thoughtful."

Elise heaved a deep sigh. "I think because sometimes when you're young, stupid, and immature, you don't quite know how to handle life's nuances, you know? A misunderstanding becomes a federal case, and the next thing you know you're hurling accusations and you're unable to trust one another, and it's easier to walk away than to think things through properly."

Shannon finished tying off the last of the beads, then hung the dress and ran a steamer across it to steam out any wrinkles. "There," she said, dusting off her hands. "As good as new. Please tell Jennifer I send my congratulations, would you? And let me know if you decide to move back home— I'd love to get together with you."

Elise nodded and leaned in to hug Shannon, holding on tightly. "Me too, Shannon. Me too."

Chapter Thirteen

ELISE was relieved to return in time to get glammed up for the wedding. She knew this makeup woman could work miracles on her tired, puffy countenance. Though how was she going to handle the complete makeover in attitude she needed to deal with Will? Will who, it turns out, wasn't a huge asshole who only thought about his own dick. But the Will who was kind, caring, and thoughtful. And maybe that extended to his dealings with Sammi Ferguson too. Hell, she'd known the girl long enough and had a pretty good idea about how Sammi usually sank her claws into some guy at every sorority function they attended. Why wouldn't that apply to weddings now too? Maybe Will was trying to be diplomatic with her and she didn't take the hint.

If that was so, why the hell would she have left the comfort of his warm bed, only to throw a little hissy fit and storm off to go back to her room and cry the rest of the night. Sometimes she didn't make much sense.

Unfortunately, there was no time now to hunt down Will and clear things up. The groomsmen were off hiking for the day while the women primped and preened and ate a catered lunch.

Luckily when Elise arrived at the suite, which was so vital for salvaging her appearance that she was starting to view it as a Red Cross tent, most of the women were done. It was kind of a bummer for the others; for the rest of the day, they had to avoid smudging their faces or messing up their hair, which look sprayed to within an inch of its life. At least Elise got a bit of a stay of execution there. Plus, she'd enjoyed some damn good muffins and edifying conversation. And maybe even found herself a new friend.

As an added bonus, it would be awfully hard for her to talk while the woman put on her face, and then with the woman styling it and the blow dryer going, again, not so easy. Because she did not want to rehash last night both at the rehearsal dinner nor what happened later. Her brain needed a drama-free zone for a while.

Which meant that naturally, the first one to accost Elise was Sammi.

"So, Elise…" she said, standing right up in her personal space and swinging her arms and hips like a kindergartener in the schoolyard. "Anything you have to tell us about last night?"

Ginger, the makeup artist, shifted as she was applying foundation, so she blocked Sammi from view, and Elise gave her a thumbs-up. Of course it didn't stop Sammi, who obviously failed to develop an understanding of social cues as a child.

"Something going on with you and the foot-long hoagie man?"

Elise tried to remain still yet so desperately had to suppress a cackle. That chick didn't forget a thing, did she?

"Like, is it as big as we all thought it might be?" She poked her head around Ginger's arm, putting her face right up by Elise's, whose lips were wrapped around her teeth with her mouth wide open, helping Ginger spread the foundation evenly. Obviously, she couldn't talk.

"What's the matter—cat got your tongue?" Sammi grinned, her teeth awfully large for that tiny body. She reminded Elise of a wolf about to eat a fairy-tale child. "Or is your tongue just tired out from last night?"

Honestly Elise would have choked had she had any sort of liquid in her throat right now.

"If you want, I could stop for a second so you can respond to her?" Ginger said.

Elise heaved a sigh. "I suppose, then maybe we can make it stop."

"Look, Sammi. I'm kinda busy right now if you haven't noticed. But even if I wasn't busy, the questions you're asking are awfully personal and I would not be inclined to answer them anyhow."

"Awww, come on, Elise. Inquiring minds want to know. You can't keep that all to yourself."

"Honey," Ginger said. "If she got a chance with something that big, who could blame her if she kept it to herself. I would!"

Sammi shrugged. "Fine. Be that way. It's not like I didn't try myself. But he shut me down stone cold."

This shouldn't give her as much satisfaction as it did, but sometimes you had to take joy in the little things. Because, well, yeah, a little side perk of Mister Montgomery was that he was hung like a horse. Praise the Lord and pass the ammunition.

Jennifer, who had been at tea with her grandma, came into the suite. "Elise—you're a lifesaver! Thank you for doing that. And I didn't even remember to ask you how you're feeling! What kind of friend am I?"

Elise reached out and clasped hands with her friend. "Only the very best kind, Jen."

"Awww, you're the best. Love you, sweetie."

She made it through the rest of her primping session relatively unscathed and was beyond happy to relax and have someone pamper her for an hour and a half.

The plan was for a champagne lunch in the suite, and then everyone would get dressed for the five o'clock ceremony, to be held at a large historic barn on a farm at the edge of Glacier Park.

The hotel wait staff had just finished serving the strawberry goat cheese and arugula salad when Jamie burst into the suite.

"Jamie—what are you doing back?"

He ran over to Jen and gave her a tight hug. He was out of breath.

"Oh God, Jen. We were almost killed by a grizzly sow." He was speaking so fast he stopped to catch his breath.

"Jesus, Jamie. Are you okay? What about the other guys?"

He licked his lips and grabbed a bottle of sparkling water that was on the table and swigged it down. "I can't believe it. All these years hiking in these mountains and never did we get attacked. I've seen my fair share of bears out there, but usually they go their way and we go ours. But not this one."

"So what happened?" Elise said. She didn't want to draw attention to the fact that she wanted to know how Will was. "Are all the guys accounted for?"

"We were on the iceberg lake trail," he said. "The one that takes you up to the snow line before you get to the icy lake, right?"

They nodded, having hiked the trail many times.

"We'd just taken a break at the big rocks and were back on the trail, the one with all the bear grass on that one side, and you have the great view of the mountains?"

The women nodded.

"No one was around, it was just our group. Will was at

the lead because the trail wasn't wide enough to walk anything but single file. Ricardo was right behind him and decided to go off the trail for a minute to take a piss. We all stopped, thank God, and while Ricardo had his back turned, a sow grizzly about a hundred yards away from us came charging down the mountain. I swear to God I nearly shit my pants." He wiped sweat from his brow before continuing.

"But Will was quick to react and grabbed his bear spray, which was clipped onto his backpack strap. Hol-y shit, he was fast. He popped that clip off and aimed it right at that momma bear and blasted it at her eyes. Stopped her like there was a brick wall in front of her and she turned and ran so fast she tripped over one of her cubs. Before we knew it, she was gone, and we knew we had to be gone equally as fast in case she returned—we'd all lost the taste for the rest of the hike. Maybe because probably half of us pissed our pants."

Elise's eyes were wide open. "You still haven't told us— is everyone okay?"

He held up his hands. "I'm getting to that bit. So Will wins the hero of the day award for his bravery in the face of some huge fucking fangs and claws that were coming at us. But unfortunately he was on the receiving end of a gust of wind that sent some of that spray in his direction. Which means some of it got in his eyes and on his skin."

Elise covered her mouth with her hand. "Oh God, is he all right?"

"Yeah, he's doing fine. We flushed his eyes with water from our water bottles and we helped him get back down the mountain since his eyes were burning like a motherfucker. He got some on his skin too, so Ricardo's got him in the ER where they're making sure he's all cleaned up, no damage to his eyes and stuff."

"Is he going to be able to be at the wedding?"

Jamie nodded. "He said, and I quote, 'Wild horses—or bears, for that matter—couldn't keep me away.'"

Elise bit her lip. They could have easily lost Will today, that quickly, in the blink of an eye, mauled to death by an angry bear, and she'd never have gotten a chance to say what she knew she needed to say to him.

"Can I go see him?"

Jamie shook his head. "They'd only let one person back with him, so we picked Ricardo since I needed to get back here anyhow. We figured the groom had to be back in time, so even if they're a bit late, the wedding can get started."

"Seriously," Jen said. "We don't care if they aren't all there on time—as long as they're all safe!"

Elise would prefer safe in her arms. But who knew if that would even be an option at this point. She'd have to wait and see.

Chapter Fourteen

"DUDE, you're my hero," Ricardo said, fanning himself like a damsel in distress as they waited in the emergency room cubicle to be discharged. "Were it not for you, my ass would've been sliced up by bear claws seventeen ways to Sunday. I'd have probably plunged a couple of hundred feet to my death when that thing tackled me. I mean, I'm kidding when I act like a girl needing to be saved, but seriously, man, thank you."

"As much as I'd like to take credit for heroic efforts, I basically did what my dad drummed into our heads from an early age. In bear country, you need to be prepared to encounter bears."

"Well, then gimme your phone. I want to call your dad and thank him for saving my ass."

Will laughed but winced. His eyes still burned and there were some patches of skin that still felt like they were on fire. He hated to think how that bear's eyeballs were feeling right about now. But he knew it was better than having to shoot her and leave behind orphaned cubs.

Will looked at his watch. "Can you find the nurse and see if we can get out of here? I didn't come all the way back to Bristol for my best friend's wedding only to miss it because I'm stuck waiting for paperwork to be filed in an emergency room."

Ricardo gave him a salute. "You got it, ace."

Will pulled out his phone and decided to give his folks a quick call. He knew the Bristol rumor mill would run rampant so he figured he'd get to them and set the record straight before his fifth-grade English teacher did.

"Mom! It's Will."

"Will, sweetie. Aren't you supposed to be at Jamie's wedding right now?"

Will nodded. "I am. Well, I will be. Not quite yet."

"Doesn't it start soon?"

"Yeah, well, we had a little thing that happened—"

"Thing? Are you okay?"

"Yes, Mom, I'm fine. We had a little bear encounter when we were out hiking this morning. Everything worked out fine, but a little bit of bear spray blew back into my eyes and stuff, so we stopped by the ER to flush out my eyes and clean up some residual oil on my skin."

"Oh, Will, I'm so glad you're safe! I'm going to put your father on."

"Mom? I can only talk for a minute."

"Will?"

"Dad?"

"Son, I hear you wrestled with a grizzly and won."

Will laughed. "Luckily you taught me what to do if I encountered a bear in the woods and I followed your wise advice. Just dealing with a little residual bear spray damage they had to clean out of my eyes."

"Son, good job staying safe and being respectful of nature."

"I owe it all to you."

"So is it true that Elise is in the wedding too?" his mother asked, trying to sound all neutral and nonchalant but failing miserably.

"How does everyone learn these things in advance but

me?"

"We have our ways. So?"

"So what?"

"So any chance for reconciliation with her?"

Will sighed. "I don't know, Ma. Believe me, I've tried. But every time I think we've moved the dial, something clogs up the gears."

"Well, it sounds to me like childbirth: one step forward, two steps back. Have patience, sweetheart. Eventually you'll get to the finish line. And it will be all the more worth it for the hard effort you put in to get there."

"I hope you're right because it's wearing me down. I don't know if I've got the patience for it anymore."

"Trust me, William. Slow and steady wins the race."

He glanced at his watch again. "I've gotta run or I'm gonna miss Jamie and Jen's wedding, and Jen will kill me, which would be ironic, considering the bear didn't manage to. I love you!"

His mother made kissing noises and his father congratulated him again for his fast thinking in time for Ricardo to return with his discharge papers.

"There's twenty bucks in it for you if you can get us back to the hotel in ten minutes."

"Throw in ten more and I'll make it in five."

"Deal."

They missed the group bus out to the property but were able to don their suits for the wedding and drive out to the venue with barely enough time to line up next to Jamie and the other groomsmen moments before Jennifer was to proceed down the aisle. Will was wiping away beads of sweat as the bridesmaids walked, single file, in advance of the bride. And just before Jennifer's appearance came Elise, breathtaking in the strapless melon full-length gown that made her tits look incredible.

He locked eyes with her warm brown ones and smiled. When she smiled back, he could have sworn there were butterflies in his stomach. Dammit, he needed badly to get her alone so he could straighten her out on whatever it was that freaked her out last night before it was too late.

Chapter Fifteen

ELISE lamented how demanding weddings could be. If she ever married, she might very well plan an elopement. Not that she was ever going to marry. But if so, none of this fifteen thousand pictures nonsense, which meant you missed out on cocktail hour and those yummy little pigs in a blanket, which were being passed around but remained out of reach, and by the time Elise had a chance to try to get some, they were all gone. At least she got herself a flute of champagne—she was going to need fortifications to get through this evening.

She kept wanting to talk to Will, but the bridesmaids and groomsmen kept being separated for all the pictures. Next, they all had to cheer on the bride and groom as they made their grand entrance as husband and wife, and then they sat down to dinner, which meant she was on one side of Jennifer at the long wedding party table and Will was on the other side of Jamie—a full three people away from each other.

At last, when dinner was over, the bride and groom did their first dance, followed by the parents, and finally—finally—they invited the wedding party onto the dance floor. But as Elise was working her way toward Will, damn if Sammi didn't beat her to it and insist on a dance with him. Which left Elise to dance with some fraternity brother of Jamie's whose eight-months-pregnant wife had to stay home so he had no one to dance with. *Whoop-de-do.*

As the song began to wind down, Will navigated his way toward her, diplomatically unloading Sammi on the guy Elise was dancing with and quickly reaching for Elise's hand.

"Care to dance?"

She grinned. "I thought you'd never ask."

He pulled her in until their bodies were pressed together, and Elise breathed into the moment, her muscles relaxing as he held her in his arms.

"I hear you got in a little smackdown with Mother Nature today," she said, winking.

"Yeah, well, a four-hundred-pound grizzly has nothing on me." He shrugged and pulled her hand close to his heart. She liked being this close, this intimate with Will. And didn't mind for a minute that they were on public display. It meant that she was finally willing to own up to what he meant to her.

"So, uh, I had a long talk with an old friend of yours this morning," she said. "And I think I owe you a rather big apology."

He turned to face her and cocked his brow. "Oh?"

"Did you know that Shannon Cadbury is a bridal seamstress?"

"I did not. Should I?"

"Nope. Just important to know that she was the person I took Jen's gown to this morning for last-minute repairs. And she was the one who told me the whole sordid truth about what happened prom night. And that you were, of course, the ultimate gentleman. So much so that you wouldn't even break her trust by telling me why you'd disappeared."

He pursed his lips and nodded.

"And it turns out I was a bit of a little shit and dug my

heels in with an indignance I don't find very flattering upon reflection."

"You were pretty entrenched."

"Can you ever forgive me for that?" She knit her brows, pleading with him to grant her mercy. "Because I don't know if I'd even forgive me. Although, if I were you, I'd forgive me because I could never forgive myself if you didn't forgive me."

"That was a lot of forgiving going on there."

She pulled him in tighter. "Does that mean you'd be willing to consider forgiving me?"

The music had changed to something up-tempo, but they continued to slow dance, nestled against one another, moving to the methodical beat of their private conversation.

"What's in it for me?"

"Hmmm… Well, you remember how I woke you up in the middle of the night the other night?"

"You mean when you thought I was an entirely different guy?"

"That's not entirely true."

"So you thought it was him *and* me? You conflated us two?" He grinned at her.

She erased the air with her hand. "Let's not worry about the finer points of that. I'm talking bigger picture here."

He lifted a brow. "You're telling me that you'd do that every night?"

She shrugged. "Fair warning: it might wear you out for your daytime hours."

"It's a sacrifice I'm willing to make."

"Well then, if that will prove to you how desperately I want a second chance and to prove myself worthy of you, then count me in."

"On one condition."

It was her turn to raise her eyebrow. "Oh?"

"Only if I can return the favor. Rumor has it"—he stroked his goatee with his hand—"you have a thing for facial hair there."

She burst out laughing. "Did I tell you that?"

"You might have blurted that out in the heat of passion."

"Let's just say I'm a big fan."

"Of me, or my beard?"

"Both."

"In that case, let's just say"—he turned to steer her off to a corner of the dance floor—"that the feeling is mutual."

Chapter Sixteen

"I am so glad you two didn't shove cake in each other's faces." Elise and Will stood hand in hand by Jen and Jamie, swaying to the music.

"And I am glad you two didn't kill each other the minute you found out you were both in the wedding."

"You know I'd not do that during your big wedding weekend. I was prepared to hold out till you left on your honeymoon." Elise grinned.

"You are aware that this was our grand scheme to get you two back together?" Jennifer fist-bumped her new husband. "Great work, babe."

"Seriously? You put that much thought into this?"

"Somebody had to!"

Will raised his hand. "I put lots of thought into it over the years. But I'd lost hope." He thrust his lower lip out. "I'm actually so glad I was in the dark about this because it would have stressed me out and I would have been thinking, rethinking, second-guessing, and being a complete fool. This way things kind of happened organically."

"I'm just glad you never completely gave up on me."

"I loved you, Elise. I couldn't do that."

She frowned. "Is that in the past tense?"

He turned to face her and reached for her hands. "We have a lot to work through still, but there is no question in my mind that I loved you then and I love you now, and I think I'll love you forever if you'll let me." He leaned in and kissed her, long and slow.

"Get a room, dude," Jamie said as he leaned over to kiss his bride.

"I can vouch for the fact that he has a room. Quite a memorable one, at that. And I'm counting the minutes till we can get back there to pick up where we left off when we were so rudely interrupted."

They all laughed as Sammi walked toward them, and Will and Elise quickly turned away before she had a chance to do any more harm.

The reception was winding down. The buses had already headed back, and only a few stragglers were hanging behind. Will had brought his car since he and Ricardo rushed there late to the wedding; Ricardo had hitched a ride back on the bus. So that left the two of them.

"Sooo…" Will said, looking up at the loft above them. "What do you say, for old time's sake? It'll be almost like we're at the prom—you're all dressed up in your evening gown, and I'm in formal wear."

"It's going to have to be quick before they turn the lights off in here."

"Caterers will be cleaning up for a while still." He grinned and grabbed her hand, pulling her toward a corner door that led to a narrow flight of steps. "Last one up there is a rotten egg."

"No fair—I've got a long dress on."

"In which case, I'll make it up to you."

A brilliant full moon shone through the cupola

windows.

Will removed his jacket and spread it out on the wide-planked wood, then gave Elise a hand so she could lie down on top of it. He sat next to her, cupping his hand to her face.

He shook his head. "I don't know how I got to be so lucky about finding a way back together again. I don't know how it happened, but I'm forever grateful for it."

She blushed. "I don't deserve someone as good as you. And you should hate me for what I put you through all these years."

He leaned forward and kissed her lips tenderly. "You know I could never hate you."

"And I should've known that you were always one of the good guys. I'm so ashamed that I behaved like such a child. My reactions—make that overreactions—were those of an immature and insecure girl. Now I'm a grown woman, full of remorse and determined to repair the damage I've inflicted. It's crazy that it took all these years—not to mention a heart-to-heart with Shannon, the object of my hurtful and misdirected wrath—to prove to me that you were a young man honor-bound not to hurt her. Back then, I loved you more than you can imagine, Will Montgomery, and now I'm realizing that my heart still swells with love for the man you've become even more so."

"Come here, you," Will said, falling alongside her, his mouth scrabbling to find hers, his hands quickly working to unzip her gown so he could lift those amazing tits out. At last, he lifted that gossamer gown of hers and found his way back home again, once and for all.

Thank you so much for reading **Bird Dog**! I hope you enjoyed it! If so, please help others find this book:

1. Help other people find this book by writing a review.

2. Sign up for my new releases email so you can find out about the next book as soon as it's available and get fun giveaways.
    http://eepurl.com/baaewn

3. Like my Facebook page.
    www.facebook.com/jennygardinerbooks

And I love to hear from readers! Let me know what you think about my books! You can write to me at jenny@jennygardiner.net, and visit me on the web at www.jennygardiner.net.

Keep reading for a sample from **Lady Killer** – the next book in the **Confessions of a Chick Magnet** series.

Lady Killer

By

Jenny Gardiner

Chapter One

COCO Lovingston was sorely tempted to bring home the adorable pink teacup pig with the black spots that someone had cruelly left in the mailbox at the Second Chances Animal rescue clinic where she worked, but she knew her landlord would kill her, not to mention her apartment neighbors, especially if the little porker turned out to be a squealer. She'd retrieved him with the day's mail, much to her surprise, and hadn't put him down for the past hour, just cuddling and kissing that sweet baby pig face.

As much as she adored animals, her living situation didn't lend itself to her taking on any sort of pet, after recently moved back from LA following a disillusioning stint trying to break into acting jobs there. She kind of hated slinking home with her tail between her legs, but if she were to be honest with herself, she was actually happy to be back in Bristol, Montana after a few years in a too-large city dealing with downright predatory industry-types who demanded sexual quid pro quos for jobs.

If one more rotten man told he she had to give him a blow job to land a pitiful little commercial spot as the "girl with herpes virus" or "girl with joint pain" in a pharmaceutical ad, her head was going to explode. She was damned if she was going to advance her career on her knees. Hell, if she was going to have a career that entailed spending a lot of times bent over, it would be to hug sweet, homeless dogs and cats that people bring into the shelter, thank you.

One condition of her return home, though, was that she wasn't going to encamp in her parents ranch outside of town; it would've been too much of a step backwards to be living in her folks' place like she was back in high school still. Enough years had passed, she knew her mom and dad enjoyed their empty-nest freedom and besides, she didn't want to deal with them monitoring her every move. So, she'd taken a small apartment in town above Vertical Drop, the ski shop on Main Street, and enjoyed walking most everywhere she needed to go. Her best friend from high school, Emma Hamilton, had recently moved back to Bristol, which meant she now had a burgeoning social life as well, so things were looking up. Now if only she could find a home for this adorable little piglet.

"You planning to do anything other than cuddle that chunk of bacon?" Tippy O'Brien, a tiny sixty-something woman with shoulder-length frizzy gray hair and bright blue eyes, said with a grin.

"Hush," she said, covering the pig's ears. "Little Oink here will get scared."

"I hate to tell you, Coco, but Oink's not going to be long for this place — we just don't have the room for a pig right now. We're already at capacity." She frowned.

Coco held the pig up right in front of the director's face. "Look at this little snout," she said, making kissy noises as she held the pigs face between her hands. "How could you ever dream of getting rid of this sweet little nugget?"

"Believe me, I'd bring in ten of them if I could, but we're just not set up for pigs to begin with, and she's going to take up the space that several dogs could occupy." She looked at her watch and tapped the face. "Clock's ticking on Oink's time here, Coco. I'm really sorry about that."

Coco thrust her lower lip in a pout. "Give me a day or two and see if I can find a good home for her."

Tippy nodded. "We'll do what we can, but please, make her adoption your priority."

"Here, hold my pig." Coco passed the pig to her boss, then pulled her long blonde hair back into a ponytail. She gave her a wink, her green eyes sparkling, and grabbed the little pig back. "I think I'll be able to do that, no problem."

By early afternoon Coco had fielded six "no's" and about four "are you crazy's", not to mention "Mommy said I can't" from one little girl. Coco could barely suppress her failure-to-adopt dismay when a tall, brown-haired man with the most striking aqua-blue eyes that reminded her of the water at Grinnell Lake in nearby Glacier National Park showed up.

She'd been sitting at the counter mindlessly braiding the front strands of her hair when he walked in and she quickly jumped up, her hair falling into her face. She quickly threw on a baseball cap to hide the mess as she greeted him. She no sooner saw him than she'd wished she'd actually put on make-up and made half an effort to look good rather than rolling out of bed, taking a long run and showing up to work sweaty with tangled hair. So much for making a decent impression on the first good-looking man to step foot into the clinic since she started working there.

"Welcome to Second Chances," she said, ushering him into the lobby. "If you have any questions, I'm happy to help. Are you here to adopt a pet?"

He nodded. "I'm looking for a kitten for my mom's

birthday," he said.

"Oh, fun. Kittens are the best. Has your mom kept a cat before?"

He shook his head. "Actually, no. My father passed away last year and he would never let her have a cat and she always kind of wanted one."

"So sorry about your dad." She frowned. "I bet your mom could use the companionship."

"To be honest, my father was a bit of a tyrant with her—he was a very old-school dominant male. Surprisingly, Mom's had a bit of a renaissance since he died. She's got a bit of a kick in her step and she's just been happier than I've seen her in years."

"Wow," Coco said. "I don't know if that is sad or joyful. I guess the latter."

"Not gonna lie. I'm pretty jazzed to see her so much happier," he said. "I mean I respected my dad, who was a hard-working rancher, but he wasn't a warm, fuzzy kinda guy. He had a hot temper and short fuse and my brother and I learned long ago it was best to avoid him altogether. We both got out of town as soon as we could and never looked back. Poor Mom didn't have that choice."

"But you're back now?"

"I've been telecommuting since I came back to help my mother settle dad's affairs, sell off the ranch and all of the assets that went with that. It was too hard to do that long-distance. Plus, I'd been living in L.A. for a while but was kind of tired of the traffic and the whole scene, so it's been okay being back in the area. I grew up in in Grundy, about an hour away from here, but we sold the ranch and I helped my mom get settled in a retirement community outside of town here—I figured there is much more for her to do in Bristol than in dinky little Grundy. There's barely a traffic light in the town."

"Well, I'm a new returnee as well, so it's nice to see someone else who got stuck returning home." She rolled her eyes.

"What're you in for?"

She laughed. "Right? Like a prison sentence. Only not really. I'm glad to be back. Grew up here. I, too, was in L.A. for a while and it just turned out it wasn't for me. Happy working with animals of the four-legged variety versus the type of predatory animals I dealt with in the entertainment industry."

"Can I apologize on behalf of the asshole men who did that?"

"Nice of you to offer but not yours to apologize for them." She smiled. "So before I take you back to the kittens, I have an idea," she said, holding up a finger. If she were to be honest with herself, maybe this felt a bit dishonest because, well, the guy was getting his mama a kitten after all. But why not a cute little pink-and-black spotted pig? She led him over to the makeshift pen they'd set up in the kennel area just for Oink. "This here's our newest addition to the clinic," she said, scooping up the tiny piglet and kissing her right on the snout. "I call her Oink. Someone left her in the mailbox, if you can believe it. I like to say she was a special delivery for the day."

He knit his brow. "Someone dropped a pig in the mailbox?"

She nodded her head. "People suck sometimes. But now she's here and I've got to find a home for her before she goes on the chopping block."

His eyes grew wide. "Seriously?"

Coco dragged her fingers across her throat, sticking out her tongue. "Can't even say she'd be destined to become bacon cause she's too little."

"Well that's just heartbreaking." He frowned. "Except I'm here for a kitten."

"Did you ever think that a cat might be a bad idea? After all, cats live a really long time. You mom might be too old to care for her eventually. We had a cat that lived to be twenty-four years old!"

He scratched his chin. "Huh… My mom would be into her eighties by then."

"And this cute little piglet would be the perfect alternative to a cat. Just think, no dander to stir up allergies. Have you ever been around cat fur?" She started scratching at her skin dramatically.

"It's true, cat fur makes me itch like crazy. But it's for her, not me—I figured cats are low-maintenance. Don't you just get a litter box and be done with it with a cat?"

"You can train this little porker with a litter box just as easily. And look at this little face." She hoisted the piglet up to his eye level. "Plus, if you need anyone to help watch Oink I'll be happy to pitch in every now and then."

"A pet pig seems crazy. But my immune system would be happier."

"I hear it's the worst, the itchy eyes, scratchy skin."

"And I get so stuffed up I can barely breathe."

"I never heard of anyone being allergic to one of these little babies."

He pursed his lips. "I'm just not sure. I mean, a pig?"

"Tell you what—if you have any issues, I'll take her back. But I'm pretty sure you'll absolutely adore her."

"And look at this baby." The piglet batted her eyelashes at him as if on cue.

He heaved a sigh. "Oh, hell, why not. Mom's already turned over a new leaf and gone for the unconventional. A pig would totally fit her new life philosophy."

She scratched her number on a sheet of paper and handed it to him. "Call me if Oink gives you any problems."

Coco decided she deserved a hike after the successful re-homing of the piglet. She was overjoyed it wasn't going to be on her shoulders that the poor baby would be put-down for lack of an appropriate home.

As she closed up the shop, she called her friend Emma, who worked as an accountant in the next town over.

"Dude. Hike. Now."

"Awww, wish I could," her friend said. "I've got to stay late to finish up a few things, so no can do."

"What fun are you? All work and no play makes Emma—"

"Makes Emma an accountant."

"Good point," Coco said. "Although I'm proud of you for having a real job, unlike some of us who can't count past our ten fingers and are instead relegated to changing cat litter boxes by the dozens and giving dogs flea baths."

"But you're nourishing your soul, so there's that. Tell you what—meet you for drinks on the rooftop at Harry's after your hike at nine o'clock?"

"That would be perfect. I need to be around humans and beer, badly. Plus, I can tell you all about the new home I found for the cute piglet, so mission accomplished for the day."

"That pig you texted me the picture of? You already found a home for him?"

"Yes, to this super cute guy who came in today."

"Huh. I never pictured the forever home for a piglet to

be with a hot guy."

"Like only ugly guys take in pigs?"

"I dunno. I mean what would a young dude want with a pig?"

"Chick magnet?"

"News flash: pigs are not puppies."

"Oink's the next best thing."

"You are super weird, you know that? But really, does the guy know it's not going to stay tiny?"

"What do you mean? It's a teacup pig."

Her friend laughed. "That doesn't mean it remains the size of a teacup. They grow up to be pigs."

"Seriously? Like big pigs?"

"I read something online one time that people buy them cause they're tiny and cute only to discover they don't stay that size and then they unload them."

"On adoption clinics."

"Yup."

"Oh shit. Like how big is big?"

"I think like three hundred pounds."

"No! That can't be."

"Google it if you don't believe me."

"Crap. I need to tell this guy before he gives it to his mother and she falls in love with it. But if I don't get out hiking now, I'll lose daylight. I'll call him first thing morning and let him know he needs to bring it back to me. I feel awful."

"Definitely let him know! Before he gets attached to the thing."

"Fine. I'm on it. Meantime see you at Harry's. If I'm not there by nine, send out the rescue squad because it'll mean the grizzlies got me."

"Nothing to joke about, Coco."

"Oh, please. I've been hiking in these woods for most of my life. Has a bear killed me yet?"

"there's always a first."

"Order me a beer and I'll see you at nine."

"Where are you going to be hiking?"

"Up near the ski resort. Gonna pick some berries and enjoy them while watching the sunset."

"Have fun! Be safe. Bring your bear spray!"

Coco laced up her hiking boots and hit the trail in the hopes of being up and back before dark. Luckily at this time of year night fell pretty late, so she'd have plenty of time. After she parked at the trailhead, she tossed her phone onto the driver's seat—no need to have that along since there was no cell service anyhow. She took a swig of her water bottle and tossed that back into the car, too—she just didn't want to lug anything extra because she was hoping she'd be able to collect huckleberries along the trails and worried the bottle might crush the delicate fruit if it banged up against the berry bag. And it was a warm enough day she dispensed with her sweatshirt as well. She did carry her bear spray, because, well, bears.

She started at the trailhead but soon began following some smaller offshoots from the trail in search of the elusive berries. She was in competition with grizzlies for the things and they tended to snarf them up for themselves far too often, not that she could blame them. But if she found enough of the delectable berries, maybe she could make a huckleberry pie and bring it out to her mom for dessert tomorrow.

Pretty soon she'd filled her bag with the juicy berries and decided she'd better find her way back onto the trail if she wanted to get to the top in time to see the sunset. But when she started to retrace her steps, she got disoriented. She'd gone off-piste, which meant there were no trail markers, so she tried to see where her feet had recently compressed the overgrowth on the forest floor, but for the life of her she couldn't tell which way she'd come from. She tried to walk toward the brightness in one direction, figuring she'd reach a clearing, but instead she found herself deeper into the woods without a clue.

She was no rookie when it came to hiking, though, and she knew to keep her wits about her and not panic. She'd be fine. She had plenty of berries and she'd find her way out in no time. Except that soon dusk was descending, and the forest grew darker and she thought the "don't panic" mantra was complete bullshit because with the setting sun, a chill soon settled over the forest, and she was alone with no sense of direction and no water and no warm clothing and nothing to eat but a bucket of berries, which she should've been dropping along the way like Hansel and Gretel with the popcorn. Now she just better hope she didn't happen upon an old woman who wanted to pop her into an oven. Or worse, a Grizzly with a hankering for huckleberry pie.

Chapter Two

ELLIOTT Barbour was no sooner out the door and driving down Main Street with a pet pig than he realized he was a damned fool for being talked into adopting a pig, of all things, for his mother. She was going to flip out over it, and not in a good way. Nothing like a little bit of buyer's remorse to kick in when you're bringing home a porcine pet for your unsuspecting widowed mom. He needed to rethink this. Clearly this was a dick-driven decision—after all, seeing that beautiful blonde chick toying with her hair when he walked in had set him on a path to make choices based on how hot she was, not on how appropriate (or inappropriate, as the case may be) the adopted animal in question might be.

He felt certain that if he'd entered the animal clinic and a seventy-year old bald man with missing teeth had tried to dupe him into a pig, he'd have told him no without a second thought. But the way that woman made that kissy-face with the piglet, it was just so damned adorable. He'd always been a sucker for a girl who loved animals, ever since he was a little kid and his father's farmhand Delilah would teach him about the animals on the ranch. Delilah was the perfect antidote to his cold father, and he learned plenty about farm-living from her that he'd never absorb from his crotchety dad.

But this took the cake. Bringing home a pig—*a pig!!*—when he went in for a kitten, all because he was so easily led around by his dick. He needed to reevaluate his priorities. Or maybe he needed to get laid, because it had been a while, at least since he'd moved back full-time to Montana. If all it took was a pretty blonde to lure him into bringing home an unwanted pig, then clearly he needed to rethink things a bit.

He checked his watch and realized the place would be closed. He wasn't going to be able to do anything about the piglet tonight. He figured he'd bring it home, try it on for size with his mother, then more than likely make the call to the woman at the adoption center first thing in the morning that he was bringing the thing back. He felt bad about it— he didn't want to see this poor creature's life cut short through no fault of her own, but he also couldn't carry that burden. *A damned pig!* He scrubbed his fingers through his hair. What the hell had he been thinking?

With Oink in the small puppy crate he'd picked up at a pet store outside of town, he entered his mom's place through the back door, slamming the screen porch as he walked inside her brand new townhouse.

"Elliott? That you?" his mom called from upstairs.

"Ma—come on down. I've got a little surprise for you."

The more he pondered this the more he knew this was the stupidest idea he'd come up with in years. He heard her footsteps as she padded downstairs. He pulled Oink out of the crate and held her up under his chin, her face pointing toward the kitchen entry way. His mother knit her brows as she walked into the room.

"What the heck are you holding a piglet for?"

"Her name's Oink. It's a surprise—your new roommate!"

His mom rubbed her brown eyes with her fists, then blinked hard, opening them wide.

"Mom? Everything okay?"

She shrugged, "I was just closing my eyes to be sure this wasn't my imagination. Because I couldn't imagine there would be a way that my son would show up with a pig for me."

Elliott reached his arms out for her to take the pig from his hands. She shook her head.

"Ma—just give her a chance. Look at how cute she is." He lifted the piglet up alongside his cheek, like they were a match set.

"Uh, I lived on a farm for a long, damned time and I am a hundred percent over dealing with farm animals, thanks. Granted we never kept a pig, but I have zero interest in doing that now." She gave first the pig then her son a little affectionate head-scratch. "I know you really can't be serious, right? This is a big joke?"

"No, it's not a joke. My plan was to find a kitten for you—I know how much you always wanted an indoor cat but Dad would never let you keep one—and somehow I came out with a piglet."

His mother burst out into laughter that made her graying bob shake. "Oh, honey. I'm afraid to ask, but was it possibly a really cute woman who talked you into a pig instead?"

He furrowed his brow. "Maybe."

She leaned over and kissed his cheek. "Perhaps that's a sign that you need to branch out and get away from your old mom and find some companionship closer to your age." She gave him a hug. "I appreciate the kind gesture. I know it's the thought that counts. And yeah, I might be more inclined toward a kitten than a farm animal, so if there's a chance of swapping it out, I'm game."

Elliott shrugged, then tucked the piglet underneath his armpit. So much for his brilliant surprise.

He pulled out the sheet of paper with the gal's number and decided to give the adoption woman a call to set in motion the return of little Oink, but his call went straight to voice mail. Oh well, looked like he was stuck with the pig till morning. After a late dinner and an hour of trying to calm down a squealing pig, he finally retired for the night, ready for a good sleep.

But somewhere around midnight he got a call from the team leader of a rescue group he was involved with that some woman had gone missing from a late-day hike, and he was needed to help spearhead an attempt to find her in the wooded, mountainous terrain.

Even though it was summertime, it could get cold at night, and beyond the hazards of freezing in the wilderness came the danger of grizzlies, mountain lions and other predators. He loaded the pig—now squealing yet again—into the crate and headed toward the rescue command center at the fire station to start assembling a search and rescue team in the hopes that they could get this lady back in a matter of hours. The pig was just going to have to come along for the ride.

Lady Killer

Coming November 26, 2019

About the Author

Jenny Gardiner is the author of #1 Kindle Bestseller *Slim to None* and the award-winning novel *Sleeping with Ward Cleaver*. Her latest works are the *It's Reigning Men* series, the *Royal Romeos* series, the *Falling for Mr. Wrong* series and her new *Confessions of a Chick Magnet* series. She also published the memoir *Winging It: A Memoir of Caring for a Vengeful Parrot Who's Determined to Kill Me,* now re-titled *Bite Me: a Parrot, a Family and a Whole Lot of Flesh Wounds*; the novels *Anywhere but Here*, *Where the Heart Is*; the essay collection *Naked Man on Main Street*, and *Accidentally on Purpose* and *Compromising Positions* (writing as Erin Delany); and is a contributor to the humorous dog anthology *I'm Not the Biggest Bitch in This Relationship*.

Her work has been found in Ladies Home Journal, the Washington Post, Marie-Claire.com, and on NPR's Day to Day. She was also a columnist for Charlottesville's Daily Progress for over a decade, and is the Volunteer Coordinator for the Virginia Film Festival.

She has worked as a professional photographer, an orthodontic assistant (learning quite readily that she was not cut out for a career in polyester), a waitress (probably her highest-paying job), a TV reporter, a pre-obituary writer, as well as a publicist to a United States Senator (where she first learned to write fiction). She's photographed Prince Charles (and her assistant husband got him to chuckle!), Elizabeth Taylor, and the president of Uganda. She and her family and menagerie of pets now live a less exotic life in Virginia.

Visit Jenny at her website jennygardiner.net and sign up for her newsletter, her blog, or find her on Facebook and Twitter. And every blue moon she'll post adorable pictures of her pets on Instagram as @thejennygardiner.